Why so much fear of tear? Because the masks we use are made of salt. A stinging, red salt which makes us beautiful and majestic but devours our skin.
Luisa Valenzuela

OTHER TITLES IN THE *MASKS* SERIES

UNDER A
CRESCENT MOON

UNDER A
CRESCENT MOON

DANIEL DE SOUZA

SERPENT'S
TAIL

The publishers thank Kathy Acker, Mark Ainley, Martin Chalmers, Bob Lumley, Enrico Palandri, Kate Pullinger, Antonio Sanchez for their advice and assistance.

British Library Cataloguing in Publication Data
De Souza, Daniel, *1945—*
  Under a Crescent Moon.
  I. Title
  823'.914[F]
  ISBN 1-85242-142-8

First published 1989 by
Serpent's Tail, Unit 4, Blackstock Mews, London N4

Typeset by Theatretexts, London

Printed on acid-free paper by
Nørhaven A/S, Viborg, Denmark

CONTENTS

To

The Turks, the most misunderstood people in the world.
My fellow prisoners in the 'Tourist Block'.
Everyone who read, criticized and encouraged.

Suzi the cat and a bird called Hope

It wasn't a real dove, just an albino pigeon with pure white feathers. Hussein and Murat, two teenage soldiers, trapped the bird and brought it to the foreigners' block. The exercise yard, roughly the size of a tennis court, was littered with prisoners soaking up the sunshine when the soldiers appeared carrying the bird which was locked in a hand-carved wooden cage. Bashfully, unsettled by the presence of so many half-naked men, they presented their gift to Sayed Ahmed.

Sayed was overjoyed. He cooed and whistled softly at the pink-eyed creature while the soldiers looked on, grinning with reflected pleasure. Then, to their utter astonishment, Sayed opened the cage door, took the bird out and threw it into the air.

"It's wrong to lock anybody in a cage, even a bird," Sayed explained gently.

At the time, no one talked about it and I thought I was the only foreigner to be moved. Prison is no place to confess such sentiments. And to empathize openly with Sayed, a Pakistani who flaunted his gayness, would have been doubly unwise.

Homosexuality was forbidden in the prison. Enforcement of the ruling was left to the lifers and long-sentence men. Punishment was usually swift and brutal. Once, as the senior European in the block, I was delegated to beat

Charlie, a young German who had been too open about his affair with Sayed. In the event, I only explained the dangers to him. Charlie spent the rest of his short sentence lying on a bunk, reading travel books.

No one ever thought of punishing Sayed. It was too dangerous. He was a lifer convicted of one murder who had already stabbed two men behind bars. But his charm was an even more effective deterrent. The balding, middle-aged Pakistani was always elegantly dressed in brightly coloured silk pyjamas. His generosity, refined manners and sensitive tact gave the whole block class. And Sayed, more than any other foreigner, had the friendship and respect of the Turkish officials, guards and soldiers. The albino pigeon was one of many gifts he was always receiving.

If only that bird had seized its freedom and flown off into the blue. Instead, it joined Oscar's flock of pigeons, sparrows and starlings waiting on the roof for their daily meals.

Oscar's devotion to his feathered friends was absolute. The plump German, convicted of raping his daughter, spent at least two hours a day crumbling bread, washing water bowls and sweeping away stale left-overs. The birds were all he ever talked about. Every morning, he rose at dawn to scatter their breakfast through a window. The birds fed in peace before the gate was opened and the courtyard became crowded with prisoners. And every evening, come rain or shine, Oscar lingered until lock-up to throw the birds their dinner, the corn kernels he scrounged from the kitchen.

There was nothing unique about Sayed's white bird, yet all the prisoners gave it a special value. It was attractive and distinctive; something bright and alive amidst the greyness.

We looked upon it as a symbol. Many of us interpreted

its decision to join Oscar's flock as gratitude to Sayed. As if the bird had opted to hang around to console him. As if it shared our passionate belief that nothing was more precious than freedom. I can't remember who first dubbed it *Umit*, Hope, but the name stuck.

To be fair, it was inspiring to watch Hope soar heavenward, float down gracefully and perch on a chimney-stack. On countless occasions when despair and misery threatened to overwhelm us, someone would sigh, "At least Hope is still with us; everything will work out."

The summer of 1983 was long, hot and deathly boring. Turkey was in the tight grip of the military. The prisons were packed and a shortage of everything from toothpaste to cigarettes nagged and irritated. The opposite block was stuffed with children; barefoot, undernourished and perpetually squalling.

If I had to sum up the wretched conditions in one word, it would be "RATS".

Hundreds of them. Swarming out from drains and cracks at night, scampering around the courtyard, flitting under bunks and crawling through pipes to enter the cells. Grey, greasy and ugly, some were as big as cats, others were so tiny they could squeeze through keyholes to reach edibles. There was no way to fight them. Sometimes the children trapped a real monster and burned it alive. But that hardly diminished their numbers.

Because of the overcrowding, many children slept on the floor. We were woken frequently in the night by their terrified screams when the rats nipped their fingers or toes. The administration, worried that a child might contract rabies, decided to shift all the kids to the clinic. In effect, the block was surrendered to the rats.

Lacking any alternative, we adapted to the rats. We

stored all our belongings and food in sacks hanging on the walls. Prisoners on the vulnerable bottom bunks slept in tightly fastened sleeping bags. We swept each cell daily to deny the animals the smallest morsel of food or crumb of bread. We survived, but we hated those rats.

Throughout the bitterly cold winter, Hope stayed with us. In the spring, it was reassuring to watch her preening in the sunshine.

Then, Mohammed found the chewed-up remnants of a rat in the courtyard. He picked the gruesome object up by the tail and gleefully paraded it around the block.

I was one of the prisoners who had suggested getting a cat to combat the rats but the idea had been vetoed by the Arab majority in the block. Cats carried disease, left droppings and were lazy. Mustafa was allergic to cats. Another claimed a friend had been smothered by one settling on his face. Claudio was the first actually to see her. The young Italian, who spent most nights moon-gazing, shook me awake, whispering excitedly, "Come and see our new friend."

Grumbling, angry at being disturbed, I climbed from my bunk and joined him by the window. My eyes had to adjust to the darkness before I saw the cat. She was a motionless shadow in one corner of the courtyard. It wasn't until she slid along a window-ledge and was illuminated by a light that I saw her properly. As cats go, she was far from appealing; small, with a long out-of-proportion body, greyish-white fur with black and brown blotches and mean, squinty, green eyes.

Watching out for her became a sudden passion of the block. Each night, a dozen foreigners sat silently by the top-floor windows, urging her on. As she stalked a rodent, we pinched each other to control our excitement, hissing fervently, "Kill it, kill it." The satisfaction of seeing her pounce on rats as big as herself was so intense, we shouted and clapped, disturbing the sleeping men.

Weeks after her arrival, the sight of a single rat was rare. They were still there, lurking under the foundations, but the cat put an end to their carefree rampage.

She was certainly wild. Unlike domesticated cats, she kept well away from humans, passing the day snoozing in the vacant block. It was a month before she deigned to make our acquaintance. We lured her out into the open with saucers of milk, which she lapped cautiously, her ears pricked to sense any danger. Only when the empty block was filled with informers and high-security prisoners did she consent to live with us. Even then she was wary. Razor sharp claws deterred our attempts to pet her and she always preferred a diet of rats to any food we offered.

The more she disdained our company, the more she appealed to us. Some Arabs continued to deny any feelings for her yet were the first to notice her absence when she disappeared for days on end. Despite their prejudices, she quickly won their admiration, if not their hearts.

She went under a number of names; *Kedi* (Cat), *Aslan* (Lion) and *Kaplan* (Tiger) were the most common. When her pregnancy became obvious, some of the men began calling her *Herospor* (Whore), and other derogatory names but most settled on Suzi, after the literary prostitute Suzi Wong.

Suzi's condition was generally frowned upon. Her job in the block was to catch rats, not to have kittens. Tolerating our celibate lives was hard enough, but Suzi's promiscuity rubbed salt into the wound and tarnished her image as an honest, hard-working friend of the block. However, we began to have long discussions on how to cope with the situation.

It was the plans for her confinement that raised emotions and triggered arguments.

With three qualified doctors in the block and my own experience in general nursing, there was no shortage of medical advice. As if that wasn't enough, it seemed as if every prisoner in the block had witnessed the birth of a baby, foal, puppy or calf and had strong ideas as to how Suzi should be treated.

A score of men squeezed into a cell and more stood in the doorway to join in the discussion. The doctors ridiculed the opinions of us lesser-educated men with their medical jargon. But the controversy didn't end there.

The height of absurdity was reached when Dr Zeki, the "fresh air" advocate, punched Dr Abdul Aziz, the "closed, calm corner" advocate, smack on the nose to settle the argument over the site of Suzi's confinement. Naturally, Suzi displayed her complete lack of respect for human expertise by choosing her own time, place and technique to give birth.

Her four cuddly kittens smoothed away our friction and even seduced the dedicated cat-haters. Only a few die-hards continued to grumble that the kittens would get under our feet and cause mess. Suzi's fame as a ratter solved the problem. Waiting for the doctor, riding in the bus to court, we boasted of her skills to Turkish friends. Desperate to de-rat their own blocks, the Turkish prisoners offered considerable sums of money for the kittens, in the belief that they would inherit Suzi's killer instinct.

Suspecting trickery, hawk-eyed foreigners watched possessively as a string of block chiefs paid us visits and handled the minute bundles of fur with awed longing.

The chiefs had been elected by fellow prisoners to represent and protect the interests of each block. Strength, size and notoriety were prime considerations.

Honesty and honour were also important but there was one quality the Turks respected above all – guile.

Ibrahim, the chief of a Kurdish block, spoke of lavish sums as he drank tea and fondled the kittens. Scratching the stubble of his outsized, fleshy chin, he haggled convincingly. Nobody saw him slip a kitten into the pouch of his baggy *shalvas*. Fortunately it mewed just as Ibrahim was leaving, otherwise we would have been the laughing stock of the prison.

It was six weeks before we reluctantly handed over the kittens to the four carefully-chosen block chiefs. In fact, none of the kittens grew up to become successful ratters, but Suzi quickly returned to the fray with a vengeance.

Apart from the usual prison dramas, life continued normally until one morning Oscar rushed in from the courtyard and raced up and down the narrow corridor outside the cells wailing, "Murder. Bloody murder."

We started up from our bunks, expecting the worst. Whose control had snapped? Who was the victim? And there was Oscar, waving a handful of blood-smeared feathers and sobbing, "Suzi's eaten Hope."

Minutes later, Suzi strolled into sight, white feathers trailing from her mouth. Stepping daintily over our toes, her tail erect, she rubbed herself lightly against our shins. We glared down at her with horror and dismay as she looked back with nothing less than smug pride.

For any other crime she would have been forgiven, but killing Hope went beyond the pale. We had to decide her punishment.

Grim and resolute, we squeezed into a cell to talk it over but all our attempts at reaching a democratic decision failed. Hardliners demanded an eye for an eye and voted for drowning. Moderates wanted the short sharp shock of a couple of slaps across her snout. Dr Zeki argued successfully against leniency with a long speech on the need to uphold biblical values. I preached my liberal, modern views and swung the vote back again. After a long day of solid discussion, we reached a compromise. Suzi's sentence was exile to a political block on the other side of the prison.

Katil (Killer), an immense tomcat, was Suzi's first replacement. About as much help as a scarecrow, he spent hours on the window-ledge watching the rats. Even when starved, it never occurred to him to eat any.

Katil was followed by *Gül*, named after a notorious murderer featured in all the newspapers. She was equally ineffectual. One cat we tested had its name changed from *Korkmaz* (Fearless) to *Korkuk* (Fearful). She hid under a bunk at the mere glimpse of a rat.

The last cat was Eve who chased and actually caught rats but, when the game was over, let them go. Watching her was so frustrating, we swallowed our pride and I was sent off to buy back Suzi.

No Sale.

Tefik, the political chief, refused to consider any deals. The lanky Marxist sneered at my offer. "You English think money will buy anything." He smirked, "You can have first pick from Suzi's next litter."

Belongings and food bags were hoisted back onto the walls. Bottom-bunk dwellers unrolled their sleeping bags. We resigned ourselves to co-existing with the rats.

Standing at a window, watching the hateful creatures flitting around the courtyard, Osama lamented, "Everything's gone wrong since Suzi ate Hope."

Arif took the words out of my mouth. "You're crazy. We're all crazy! Hope was just a dumb bird."

Lynus and Yilmaz

During my third year in prison I worked in the clinic where a twist of fate introduced me to Lynus and Yilmaz and probably saved my life.

My job was nursing and cleaning. I was the do-all for a floating population of malingerers, three *Ahgalar*, wealthy godfatherish criminals, and a dozen *Kabadailar*. The *Kabadailar*, which literally means "uncles of force", were the bodyguards of the *Ahgalar*. They were handsome, strong young men who spent their days in wide-lapeled suits, slouched, brooding in corners.

Anarchy ruled the prison and the corridors were no-man's land. Gangsters stalked or hid from *hasem*, enemies; packs of Fascists and Marxists fought for power. Many prisoners carried fourteen-shot automatic pistols. The guards were unarmed. Despite the violence and almost weekly riots, the clinic was left in relative peace. It was in everybody's interest that it continued to function.

There were never more than six genuinely sick prisoners in the clinic. They were mostly old men dying of cancer, as all the badly injured men went straight to the outside hospital. However, within months I became an expert in stab wounds, able to decide quickly whether stitches or an X-ray were needed. It was exhausting but the work got me through a bad patch when life

15

didn't seem worth living. My only friend was Fellek, a hunchbacked Armenian teenager. He helped out and brewed the tea, but my Turkish was still too limited for me to talk much with him.

The clinic had forty steel-barred cells on two floors of two back-to-back blocks. Narrow corridors separated the cells from windows stretching the entire breadth of the blocks. The cancer patients occupied the ten bottom-floor cells leading away from the main door. Visitors sniffed the disinfectant-doused corridor, glimpsed the grey-faced, doomed men and departed rapidly, leaving the upstairs *Ahgalar* to enjoy their comfortable seclusion.

At the back of the clinic were ten cells reserved for potential suicides. Intended as a peaceful oasis away from the violent prison dormitories, the cells were sordid and depressing. They were bare, dark and dank with dripping pipes sagging away from the ceilings – an invitation to the occupants to hang themselves. The stretch of corridor outside the cells was a slum alley. It stank of urine. A solitary lamp cast eerie shadows.

The shattered windows of suicide alley overlooked the courtyard of the fascist block opposite. The fascists were fifty Grey Wolf right-wing Turkish nationalists, always sleek and fit on a nourishing, plentiful diet provided by outside sympathizers.

Early each morning, the Wolves marched up and down the courtyard in an exaggerated goose-step to the beat of coarsely-bellowed martial songs. As they marched, I checked the suicide cells. Sometimes, I found an occupant swinging lifelessly from a makeshift rope. Macabre humour was necessary to ward off depression. Entering each cell I used to chirp cheerfully, "Good morning" or wisecrack, "This could be your lucky day." The silent, ragged men, mainly child-killers and molesters, eyed me with uncomprehending despair.

16

Before beginning my cleaning chores I usually paused to smoke a cigarette and watch the Wolves march. Secure behind the iron barred windows, I fell into the habit of bawling out, "Ein, Zwei, Drei, Vier."

Three days before Sheker Bayram, a festival that concludes the month-long fast of Ramazan, I became ill. Fever, vomiting with diarrhoea; a dramatic display of the human defensive metabolism that at most would have gone on for twenty-four hours. Normally prisoners were left to sweat out such illnesses but Head Guard Kasim generously decided to shift me to the hospital as an emergency case.

The secure ward of the hospital occupied the top floor of a six-storey building, just outside the prison. From the windows it was possible to look over the twenty-five foot high walls around the jail. I had hardly been there an hour when sirens began howling.

At the time I was too ill to care, and it wasn't until later I heard the Wolves had hacksawed their way into the clinic. Armed with pistols and knives, their main aim had been to kill Halim, a paralysed Marxist militant, but they had also planned to settle with me. They succeeded in murdering Halim but, finding me gone, had only destroyed my cell.

The following morning I woke up brimming with life after a night on a glucose drip to see Lynus and Yilmaz sitting at the end of my bed. Their expressions of concern were so sincere, I laughed to show my good health. Lynus Thomas was a forty-year-old Irishman, all five feet of him as hard as nails from twenty years as a London navvy. He had protruding ears and goofy teeth poking through an idiot's grin. He claimed to be on the run from a posse of lusting women. Supposedly, one admirer had followed him all the way to Turkey. Despite his clownish looks, I believed him.

Serving two years for offering a joint to an undercover cop, Lynus was in hospital because of an ominous chest growth. He was finishing his third month in the secure ward.

Yilmaz Güney was then about forty-two, wiry, lithe and dynamic. His intelligent, humorous eyes exuded the youthful charisma that had made him Turkey's greatest film star and director but his face was deeply lined and his hair had turned steely grey. Serving eighteen years for the political murder of a judge, he was being treated for tuberculosis. The disease had eaten deep hollows into his cheeks. He was never still. Always he vibrated with nervous energy.

I don't think Lynus understood who Yilmaz was. He accepted men as he found them, never questioning their background. They were sharing a small corner room at the end of the corridor, crowded with stacks of English and Turkish books.

For all his self-characterization as a manual worker, Lynus's general knowledge was second to none, and on the subject of Irish literature he could hold his own against an Oxford don.

That first evening Yilmaz clearly resented my company but seemed to understand that Lynus was obliged to invite me into the room and welcome me as a fellow Londoner. The time was spent very quietly, squatting on the floor reading. On either side of me, the two men were reclining on their beds engrossed in books. Periodically, they'd rise and cross the small room to underline passages in each other's books. It took me some time to realize both men were reading Oscar Wilde's *Ballad of Reading Gaol*, Lynus in English and Yilmaz in Turkish.

For Yilmaz, that hospital room possibly provided the only sanctuary from fame he ever enjoyed behind bars.

In all his films he had been the hard, brave man, fighting and invariably dying for honour. Volatile and temperamental, he complained of being constantly tested by other Turkish prisoners curious to discover if he was as tough as his screen image. Being a living legend locked up with his admirers was an unremitting ordeal.

I was tolerated that first visit. By the second day, even Lynus ignored me and I felt like an interloper. They each had books by the same authors beside them – Wilde, Shaw and Joyce. The to-ing and fro-ing between beds was more energetic, punctuated with crude insults in their respective languages.

Yilmaz slapped his book down and snarled in Turkish, "You piss-stained heathens think you're so smart but you have no passion." Lynus grinned, shook his finger and lectured back in a thick Irish brogue, "Now tell me, how is a barbarian going to understand such an Irish genius, *Eshek.*"

I was shocked. *Eshek* (Donkey) was the only Turkish swear word Lynus knew. However mild, it still struck me as a dangerous insult to direct towards a fiery character like Yilmaz.

But Yilmaz just grinned and affectionately cuffed Lynus before delivering a Turkish curse in reply.

I badly wanted to befriend them enough to enter their literary dialogue but the matron had other plans for me.

Melda Hanum was not the kind of woman to mince words. The proportions of her slim body were defined, with black underwear clearly visible through a thin white tunic. Her painted and plucked features were set in the mould of a Hollywood starlet. But above all she was the matron, with an icy professionalism that terrified me into subservient obedience.

There was no choice in the matter. Being a healthy

male and a clinic cleaner to boot, my stay in the hospital depended on how well I worked to prepare everything for the coming festival. Just one lapse and I'd be back in jail that same day.

Equipped by Hamid, the wheezy, ancient civilian cleaner, I was soon down on the floor scrubbing every inch of the hospital as if my life depended on it. I was so frightened of angering Melda Hanum that I worked right through to lunch without a break. It didn't need brains to recognize the benefits of passing Bayram in hospital. Just the meals and sight of pretty young nurses was sufficient to curb my usual sloppy work habits. It took me until late at night but, by the time Melda Hanum was satisfied, every window and floor in the hospital was polished to perfection.

Passing the corner room on my way to bed I noticed the light was on and popped my head round the door to say goodnight to Yilmaz and Lynus. They were still at it. Yilmaz was bending over Lynus's English copy of *Ulysses* to underline a paragraph and compare it with his own Turkish edition. They were so busy they failed to notice me and I quietly slipped away.

The next morning, most of the patients rose early and got themselves spruced up in suits to greet the dignitaries. It was the beginning of Sheker Bayram, an important day. The Military Commander, the Prison Governor and the Head Doctor swept through the doors surrounded by their flunkies. First they clustered round the beds of the gravely ill cancer patients, some of them only hours from death. Offering consoling comments, they lingered and mourned.

The male nurses hovered in the back row of the huddle and secretly sold alcohol. Many of the prisoners, standing stiffly in line to be inspected by the VIPs, extended one hand to shake while clenching a concealed raki bottle with the other. By evening the whole ward was in a gregarious, inebriated mood.

Out of thirty-odd patients, fewer than ten could be described as needing hospital care. The rest were *effendis*, men who had bribed their way onto the ward.

The size of the bribes depended on the time of year, the most costly being Sheker Bayram, when up to 50,000 lire was paid to be hospitalized. The patients were naturally a very select group and included some of the most notorious figures from the Turkish criminal fraternity. Lustre was added by half-a-dozen society criminals including a judge, a surgeon and an ex-cabinet minister.

I was taking drunken fantasy strolls with Lynus right across London when Yilmaz staggered over with Hassan Heybetli and Kurt Idris. More bandit than gangster, they were the ambitious sons of Kurdish chieftains who ruled vast areas of the eastern mountains. Idris was bland but Hassan was animal-ugly, as if exploding with inner rage. A very wild man.

I don't know what Yilmaz had said, but the three men sat before Lynus as if meeting a guru. In those days my Turkish was far from fluent, yet Yilmaz insisted I should interpret everything Lynus said.

He was fascinated by Lynus's tales of building motorways and skyscrapers. He couldn't get enough translations of what it was like to be a London paddy. I did my best communicating the nuts and bolts of second class citizenship and Yilmaz immediately embellished my efforts in Kurdish for Hassan and Idris.

Finally, his intense questioning became too tiring and, when he huffed at my poor command of Turkish, I wove drunkenly back to bed.

The next morning, just before the visiting period for

family and friends began, disaster struck. Overnight the toilets had rebelled and the entire corridor was spotted with turds bobbing in a lake of waste water.

Hamid couldn't be found and there wasn't a male nurse in the building. Melda Hanum sniffed haughtily, "You'll have to clear it up yourself."

All the *effendis* in their smart suits growled and cursed. None had any desire to strip off and clean up toilet waste. Time was passing. Within an hour the first visitors would arrive. Inevitably attention focused on me.

Having a healthy clinic cleaner in the ward must have struck them as divine providence. First came the charm, then threats and finally bribes. I may have been a heathen swabber but I knew my rights.

The deal was that I'd clean their corridor in double time but, as payment, I demanded hashish.

Melda Hanum stiffened and puffed up with indignation, then capitulated under Hassan's vicious sneer. The tribe of *effendis* nodded and grinned so I began to work.

The initial job was clearing the toilets and, by the time they were flushing, Lynus had delivered the first joint.

At the end of the corridor Yilmaz sat perched on a high stool overlooking the flood. Twenty of Turkey's top criminals, dressed to kill, gathered in doorways observing the operation.

Pyjamas rolled up to my knees, using a bed-pan as a tool, I tried to scoop up the unsightly turds. I was less than successful. The flow of water kept carrying them out of reach. Then Lynus, braying laughter, paddled to my assistance and together we began to make headway.

High above us, Yilmaz would spot an elusive turd, pointing it out with a broom handle and shouting seaman-style the equivalent of "heave to starboard, heathen". Belligerent faces cracked into smiles. Melda Hanum was openly grinning!

The subsequent days were gentle but sad. Lynus was dying. It was no longer possible to hide the fact that his symptoms were overtaking the effectiveness of the drugs. He was in permanent pain.

Floating on a daily cocktail of opiate-based injections, he infected the hospital with his irreverent yet saintly Irish humour. As far as the doctors, nurses and most of the patients knew, he was just another bit of flotsam disgorged by industrialized Europe. A drug-obsessed heathen, and worthless, but fun to have around. His constant lament in primitive Turkish, *"Esrar yok; hiyat yok"* – No cannabis: No life – invariably provoked chuckles but it was more the poignancy than the humour.

He knew he was dying, that the Turks were humoring him with an elaborate treatment based on placebo pills. But to save their feelings he only talked about it to Yilmaz and his more discreet friends.

Lynus laughed at my anger when I cursed the doctors for letting him die.

"They mean well and they're magnificent actors. It would be impolite to spoil such a convincing performance."

I was very moved and impressed by his relaxed acceptance of mortality. It wasn't the unnerving indifference of most dying people. Lynus was living every moment to the full. Death was only a cigarette break, an interval in an on-going show.

Throughout the ward there was one all-pervading thought... "get Lynus home."

Lynus continued the pretence of optimism with his doctors but to us spoke openly about death. Dublin, London or Istanbul, he didn't give a damn. He could die just as well anywhere in the world. The more he protested, the greater our determination. Lynus had to be flown home.

Brancaleone bore the brunt of our obstinate demands. He was Lynus's consul, a third-generation Maltese-Turk, holding a British passport by an accident of history. Short and balding, he made unconvincing excuses. He was doing his best. The lawyers had been working on it for a month. Daily, the harried man departed from his visits beneath an onslaught of the most evil glares in Turkey.

He was fortunate. I had to live with the post-visit inquests.

The *effendis* to a man wanted to be good Muslims. Costs were immaterial, the court had agreed, why wasn't *my* country flying him home?

That Britain dared prevent them from fulfilling a religious duty shocked them profoundly.

Yilmaz, camped outside the corner room, put it into Turkish terms. Lynus was compared to a Kurdish migrant worker who had recently died in a Berlin prison.

According to Brancaleone, the delay was purely bureaucratic. The papers were all in order but none of his normal contacts dared put them into action. The problem was to get the General Prosecutor, Head Doctor and Prison Security Colonel together to sign the exit papers. They were all busy men.

Leaving after one afternoon visit to the corner room, Brancaleone found his route blocked by Yilmaz. For a few minutes they disappeared into the kitchen. Both emerged looking determined and confident.

Yilmaz was unbearable for two days. Insisting on doing his *volta*, exercise walk, alone, his pace up and down the corridor was almost a trot. Hassan and Idris crouched in doorways to ensure his solitude was uninterrupted.

On the third day, when Brancaleone next visited, the ward had an expectant air. Yilmaz, Hassan and Idris, wearing their smartest suits, were joined by the consul for tea. They only talked a few minutes, then the consul hurried off without even seeing Lynus.

From the window, I saw him leaving the hospital and began to understand. He walked towards a shiny finned Cadillac adorned with superfluous grilles and lights. From the slouching stance and muscular build of the waiting chauffeur, I guessed it was one of Hassan's cars. Brancaleone climbed into the back of the vulgar but impressive machine and all the patients lined the windows to watch it glide off to join the Istanbul traffic.

Late afternoon the Cadillac returned. Brancaleone climbed out first, followed by three other men. Their clothes and gait identified them as the General Prosecutor, Head Doctor and Prison Security Colonel – three of the most powerful and important men in Turkey. The stony-faced chauffeur, unimpressed, herded them into the hospital like a flock of sheep.

The visitors were obviously nervous as they passed the gauntlet of impassive patients. Yilmaz swung the door of the corner room open without offering a word of greeting.

They left minutes later. Brancaleone nodded to me, bemused, "He'll be in London tomorrow morning."

Lining up to hug Lynus goodbye, we were all crying. Lynus punched me playfully and laughed, "Cheer up. With me gone, Melda Hanum might fancy you."

When Hassan tried to give him a locket holding a tiny Koran, Lynus joked, "You keep it. With your life-style you'll be needing it."

Yilmaz had his arm around Lynus's shoulders, weeping like a baby as he led him downstairs.

Watching them until they disappeared from sight, my own feelings bewildered me. Lynus was going home to die – yet I envied him.

Later I understood.

I was jealous of the love he had shared with Yilmaz.

Turan

"Geh vedi, geh vedi, cos here I com."

There was something odd about the thin, wailing voice singing the refrain repeatedly. It took me several minutes, hovering between sleep and wakefulness, to solve the puzzle. The words were barely English, the melody distorted, yet I recognized it as the chorus line from the American hit song 'Get Ready'. Once it had been a favourite and hearing it again after so many years, I felt a rush of nostalgia.

But who could be singing such a song on a winter's morning in a Turkish prison? Reluctantly, I left my warm nest beneath a pile of blankets and ventured out of my cell into the icy, draughty corridor.

The sound came from outside the block, yet when I first peered down into the courtyard, it looked empty. Then I saw a tiny figure huddled in the only corner touched by the watery dawn sunshine. A shorn head poked out from a shapeless, outsized jacket. The child was a new arrival at the juvenile block facing the foreigners' wing. He was trying to shield his bare feet from the cold by drawing them up inside his thin prison-issue trousers.

Returning to my cell, I rummaged through boxes of belongings for old socks, a sweater and a pair of plastic shower sandals. I took them down the stairs to the courtyard gate and called through the bars to the boy.

He could hardly control his shivering hands long enough to put on the socks. When he stripped off his jacket to don the sweater, I glimpsed his emaciated chest. His ribs protruded so starkly that he looked deformed. His fingers were covered in chilblains. At a guess, he was no more than eight years old with features showing him to be an *arap*, mixed blood. The whites of his eyes contrasted strongly with his dark complexion.

Having put on all the clothes, he flashed such a wide grin, I had to ask, "Are you hungry?"

I only had milk and biscuits to offer but he wolfed them down. In a spray of crumbs, he told me his name was Turan and his crime was the theft of two oranges. Incredulous, I asked, "Two oranges?"

"Well, I've only got two hands. I couldn't carry more," he replied flatly.

He told me that he was eleven years old and showed me his prison identity card. Then, having looked round cautiously to see if anybody was watching, he took out an old plastic wallet from his trouser pocket and extracted his most prized possession, a Polaroid photograph of a hefty black GI cradling a baby.

"He's my Dad, holding me when I was little," he said, proudly.

That explained the American pop song. "Did he teach you English?" I asked.

Turan scowled and mumbled softly, "Not much. I was only six when he left." Then, more cheerful, "When I'm bigger he's going to come back and take me home. To the United States of America."

He hesitated over "home". He sounded awed by the United States of America. This was his dream for the future.

He hardly mentioned his mother. From different

28

remarks pieced together, I understood she had deserted him when he was still very young. Since then, he had been living in an uncle's garage where he worked as an apprentice mechanic.

"Don't you go to school?" I asked. "School!" he answered scornfully. "I've never been near one. I'll learn to read and write when I get to America."

His story was familiar. Although attendance at primary school was compulsory, the law was rarely enforced. Parents on starvation wages couldn't afford school uniforms, books and pencils. Similarly, there were laws forbidding child labour but the pittance earned by children helped families survive.

Matter-of-factly, Turan described how his uncle, unable to afford the expense of keeping an extra child, had taken him to the Izmir State Orphanage. Turan had spent several hours exploring the spacious grounds, romping with other orphans, before being interviewed by the administrators.

His delight in recalling what must have been an intensely enjoyable experience suddenly vanished. Shaking his head with baffled despair, he choked, "They wouldn't take me. I don't know why." After a long silence, on the verge of tears, he turned aside to hide his face.

I also had to turn away – to hide my anger. I thought my years behind bars had toughened me but the kid's story of being excluded even from an orphanage was too cruel.

By then, some of the other children had emerged from the block and were crouching in the sunlit corner of the courtyard. Turan eyed them apprehensively.

The kid deserved a break. I saw Orhan stumbling sleepily into the yard and called out to him.

Orhan, barely sixteen, had already served four years

in the juvenile block for armed robbery. Extremely tough and vicious, he was feared even by the guards. The administration had made him chief of the juveniles, hoping that the responsibility would blunt his rebellion.

Orhan swaggered over. The hand on his hip gripped a knife concealed under his shirt. Turan took one look at him and sidled fearfully away.

I offered Orhan a cigarette. He planted it in the corner of his mouth where it accentuated his ugly sneer. Despite the bitter cold, he wore only a t-shirt and pyjamas. With his bare arms crossed to display crude pictures of a knife and pistol, tattooed in the prison with inked razor blades, he slouched against the bars.

We began with the usual small talk. Then I pointed to Turan. "He was delivered this morning. I want you to go easy on him."

Orhan's sneer widened into a cocky grin. "What's in it for me?"

I gave him the almost full packet of cigarettes. "That's just a start."

He slipped the cigarettes into his pocket and drawled, "It's OK with me, but what about my friends?"

I knew what he meant. The sodomy rites with which juvenile prisoners initiated newcomers to their block were common knowledge throughout the prison. The kids' crude jokes portrayed the ritual as a manhood test. Living opposite the juveniles, the foreigners were often woken in the night by the muffled, agonized screams of kids being raped. They all seemed to recover quickly yet it was important to me that Turan should be spared such torture.

Orhan sensed my concern. He threatened ominously, "There'll be no problems in the future but I can't guarantee tonight."

I looked him straight in the eye. "You can do better

than that, Orhan. You're responsible for the block. If Turan passes a peaceful night, there'll be no trouble. If anybody wakes him, you'll regret it." I reached out to grasp his t-shirt and pulled him violently against the bars. "Don't forget what happened to Tana."

The story of Tana, a teenager murdered in Istanbul Prison, was known throughout Turkey. Tana and his gang of knife-toting juveniles had terrorized adult inmates, operating a shakedown racket in the corridors. When it got out of hand, the prisoners hired a professional killer to shoot him. It would have taken only a word to the politicals or a little money in a *Kabadai*'s pocket to have Orhan similarly dealt with. I wasn't bluffing and Orhan knew it. There were no screams that night.

The juvenile block was the most deprived and sordid wing in the prison. Aged between eight and seventeen, one hundred and twenty children lived in a block equipped with thirty-eight bunks, two toilets and one tap. They had no chairs, tables or cupboards, only a television.

Loaves of bread and two tanks of watered-down vegetable stew were thrust through the door each day. They became the instant focus of a desperate scramble. Lacking spoons or plates, the younger children pounced wildly on the tanks, scooping up the scorching stew with their fingers. In a frenzy, they stuffed their mouths to bursting point before the fully-grown juveniles kicked them away.

Once a fortnight, the whole block was herded off to the bath-house. With great whoops and whistles, they filed out of the block and down to a domed, tiled basement *hamam*. Issued with bars of primitive soap, they had ten minutes to wash their bodies and uniforms. Without towels or dry clothes, they returned shivering

31

like drenched kittens. The showers weren't much help. The block teemed with lice, rats and cockroaches. Many of the children suffered from skin diseases and they had no money to buy the ointments prescribed by the prison doctor.

Orhan took care of Turan and grew fond of him. Although virtually a slave to the tattoo-scarred block chief and his gang of mini-thugs, Turan was fortunate. He received enough food, ate from a plate with a wooden spoon and had clean bedding. Over the next three months he thrived. He grew at an astonishing rate, filling out, attaining a lean, healthy sleekness until he was scarcely recognizable as the undernourished wretch I first encountered. He proved to be a promising footballer. Scampering barefooted after the rag ball, he learnt to swerve, dribble and pass skilfully.

The kids' spirits never failed to amaze me. Despite their miserable conditions they were always boisterous and enthusiastic, singing, shouting and playing away the days. They had no real contact with jailhouse discipline. Once a week the *hoja*, teacher, visited and lectured them on morality and religion. The entire block was made to squat silently in the courtyard by truncheon-carrying soldiers while the black-bearded *hoja* talked. Turan became an expert at disrupting the lessons, catapulting paper darts to sting the back of the *hoja*'s neck. Frequently he felt the lash of the *hoja*'s strap but, because of his size, the strokes were less violent than those used on the older boys.

During those first three months Turan's personality also filled out. He became more confident, cheerful and talkative. He lost his fear of prison and began to enjoy the comradeship and unruly life. He also began to ape Orhan's swagger and curses. In the spring of 1981 he was released from prison. Two weeks later he was back on a burglary charge.

Dressed in a flashy new shirt and expensive shoes, bought from the proceeds of burglaries, he was welcomed back by Orhan like a younger brother. He was the same dreamy kid, inventing complex stories of how his father had written to summon him to America and how his uncle, jealous and fearful of losing a worker, had destroyed the letter. Again, he became popular amongst the kids by terrorizing the *hoja*.

However naughty, he remained sweet-natured, with a strong sense of justice and personal honour. When the other children trapped a rat and were dangling it over a fire in the courtyard, Turan stopped the slow torture by killing it outright with a brick. One night he braved the anger of the older juveniles, shouting for the guards to halt the ritual rape of another kid. Whenever Orhan called him, Turan immediately rushed to his side. He became Orhan's knife-keeper, ensuring the weapon was always sharp, clean and instantly available. The children feared Orhan, so Turan, his knife-keeper, was also someone to be approached with caution. As Turan's prestige rose, his devotion to Orhan was more apparent. One day, his hero-worship cropped up in a conversation I had with Prosecutor Shefki Levent.

Shefki Levent was in charge of Shrinigar, one of the three specialized juvenile detention centres in Turkey. An ageing yet dynamic man, he was renowned for his liberal and humanitarian views. Shefki often visited our block to practise his English. All the foreign prisoners looked on him as a friend.

From the window of our block he stood watching Turan playing football in the courtyard. Frowning, he sighed, "I wish I could take him with me. None of these kids should be here. But there's nothing I can do.

33

Shrinigar is overcrowded. Besides, to be considered he'd have to be sentenced and, without money for a lawyer, we can't bring his case to court."

One outcome of Shefki's visit was that Orhan and two older boys were switched to an adult block and had no further contact with Turan.

For a time, Turan was calmer. He even started the informal literacy lessons. I convinced him that, with an education, he'd be able to work in a bank where he could steal far more money than any bank robber – enough to fly to America. The idea caught on. A dozen illiterate kids gathered each morning beside the courtyard gate, where I gave them lessons in writing, reading and arithmetic. They all had the same ambition – to leave prison and become bank clerks.

The lessons didn't continue for long. Too many children hung around interrupting the classes. Halef, the teenager appointed by Shefki as the new block chief, didn't have Orhan's sense of leadership. He was too lenient and unconcerned. Turan and some other kids were always challenging his authority. There were constant fights and uproar.

The noise the kids made was overwheming so I talked with the prosecutor. I tried to persuade him to open the prison school. He let me talk and then answered, "You don't understand. Officially, there are no children in Turkish prisons so how can I open a school for children who don't exist?"

A week later, minutes before a group of Justice Ministry officials arrived to inspect the foreigners' living conditions, the prosecutor ordered the children's eviction. It made no sense until Head Guard Jasim Baba told me, "He has to. If the Justice Ministry men look out any window of your block and see the state of the kids, it would cause no end of trouble."

The juveniles ended up in a disused basement workshop, with no bunks or courtyard for exercise. Two months passed before they returned to the block opposite the foreigners.

Over the next five years, conditions for the juvenile prisoners improved considerably. Teenage inmates were transferred to another block away from the youngsters so there was no more male rape. A school was opened for the adult prisoners but the kids were also made to attend. However, hygiene, health, clothing and food problems were never solved.

My friendship with Turan slowly lost its warmth. He joined the gang of tough kids who skived off from the prison school where I worked. He was in and out of prison half a dozen times for assorted misdemeanours. At the age of fifteen, he moved to the block for teenage inmates and I didn't see him for more than a year.

When I next met him, Turan was a strapping seventeen-year-old. I was walking down the corridor with Head Guard Ismail and Turan rushed straight into us. Ismail went on, leaving me standing alone with Turan. "That was close," he winked. "If he knew what I've got here I'd be in the slammer." He flashed his uniform jacket open to show me the bottle of codeine cough-mixture fixed under his belt. I saw the outline of a flat knife at the back of his hip.

"Where're you bunking?" I began. "What's the rap this time?"

"Right now I'm still with the juveniles, but next week they're shifting me to Ibrahim's," Turan grinned with pride. Sensing my disbelief at his mention of the block reserved for hardened criminals and lifers, he went on, "This time I'm on a mugging rap. The bitch had to be stitched up so they're throwing the book at me. But

I'm still under age." He shrugged, "They can't give me much."

Leaving him, I remembered a sick friend in with the juveniles. "By the way, Sadik's in your block. You owe me one. Give him a message, will you?"

"What's in it for me?" He gave me a shrewd glance.

I remembered that first morning when Turan had squatted shivering in the courtyard, singing to himself.

"You're right," I conceded. "You don't owe me anything."

The school

Prosecutor Emin Bey's opposition to the school was not overt. He was far too experienced to oppose a Justice Ministry directive. Burly and thuggish, with a gambler's swagger, he was the first civilian prosecutor to regain command of a high security jail, just three years after the 1980 military coup. Satisfying both generals and politicians was a difficult task but Emin Bey was one of the few prosecutors who managed to avoid criticism.

He was renowned throughout Turkey for being a tough man, able to make the most recalcitrant prisoner toe the line. His guiding principle was always to keep prisoners reined in as tightly as possible. Any unlocked block door was an invitation to rioting; operating a school would have cracked his security system wide open.

When the Prosecutor first received instructions from the Justice Ministry to open the school, he exaggerated the problems. "With three and a half thousand men, women and children, every day is a crisis. More time, guards and money are needed. Then the school can open," he told journalists from local newspapers.

The Prosecutor had more difficulty restraining Mustafa, the young education director. He failed to recognize the depths of Mustafa's determination.

Mustafa was a polite, softly-spoken man whose

patience never faltered. He was small and neat with rodent-like features and a bristling moustache.

Mustafa was always seeking to outwit the Prosecutor. He could have complained directly to the Justice Ministry about the absence of a school; at the very least, that would have lead to an investigation. Making such a complaint himself would have been subversive and disloyal but there was nothing to stop a *prisoner* sending a petition.

The catch was that all appeals and petitions to the Justice Ministry had to be typed, rubber-stamped and countersigned. Emin Bey controlled the stamp and added the signatures.

When Mustafa asked me to paint Ataturk's famous slogan, *"Ne mütlü Türkum diyene"* – How happy I am to be Turkish – above the door of the juvenile block, I had no idea what it would lead to.

The ladder was rock steady. No need for Mustafa to hold it while I worked. He stood there whingeing about the Prosecutor's obstinate refusal to sanction the school or forward an appeal to the Ministry. Concentrating on signpainting, I only half listened. "You should ask Aydin," I suggested to silence him.

"Now why didn't I think of that?" Mustafa agreed, a shade too hastily.

My friendship with Aydin dated back half a decade. As the most powerful trustee prisoner in the jail, he was very unpopular. He ingratiated himself with the administration and irritated guards and prisoners alike with his superior, scholarly airs. However, Aydin was also highly respected. He was, after all, the genius who had carried out Turkey's biggest banking fraud. I found his refined manners an intriguing change from those of the crude, macho inmates. He was a useful friend. A tall, gaunt man, it was Aydin who had arranged for my appeal for transfer to an open prison to bypass the Prosecutor and go directly to the Ministry.

Less than a week later, Mustafa called me to our block door and gave me a sheet of paper. "Here's that appeal *you* needed." He was gone before I had a chance to speak.

The appeal was a masterpiece, ostensibly written by a repentant terrorist who, in the humble, beseeching style favoured by the Ministry, pleaded for a chance to finish his education.

Passing the single page to Aydin was easy. He smiled and nodded as I explained the problem. I don't know how he obtained the Prosecutor's signature and stamp but, for a man who had swindled millions from under the noses of suspicious bank directors, it must have been child's play.

The Ministry's answer came nine months later. I was called to the door and Mustafa's grinning rodent face peeped absurdly out of his outsized overalls. Surrounded by a sea of children, he chirped, "More painting to do."

I understood. Permission to open the school had been granted.

Some of the guards and soldiers resented the giggling excitement of the kids and were angry as we trooped past them up the corridor. But old-timers nodded their approval. Jasim Baba tested the arm muscles of a tiny ten-year-old newcomer, joking, "You won't be much use. Where did you find the strength to pick pockets?"

When we reached the rooms, our elation dimmed. They hadn't been used for years. Everything was coated in filth. Doors hung off their hinges. After nearly a day's scrubbing and cleaning, we had eliminated the worst of the dirt but the rooms still looked dilapidated, with peeling walls and broken furniture.

We needed paint and timber urgently. Mustafa

moaned pitifully, "All the Prosecutor will give us is worthless promises."

I was aggressively scrubbing the dirt-ingrained floorboards. Mustafa knelt down beside me and started one of his aimless natters about the mountain of equipment being used to renovate the Izmir courthouse. "All that money! It's disgusting." He sounded bitter.

"You know what?" he added lightly. "Your friend Aydin is doing the paperwork on that job."

I fell for it. "We could ask him again." I lowered my voice. "He steals millions by shuffling paper. We only need a few planks and a spot of paint."

Mustafa was shocked. "You can't do that. It would be theft!" He gave me a frightened grin and whispered, "Do what you like but don't tell me anything."

It worked. The paint and wood arrived in a military ambulance. Not long afterwards, the Prosecutor took Aydin out of his comfortable sinecure and transferred him to the open prison. "He knows I did it but he can't work out how," Aydin boasted cheerfully as he said goodbye.

The rough planks were transformed by the prison carpenters into polished desk tops and benches which were both comfortable and functional. The freshly painted classrooms gleamed invitingly despite being institution grey. Even the dour portraits of Ataturk which hung in all four rooms hinted a smile.

Mustafa pretended to be unimpressed. Catching me taking a break with my gang of child labourers, squatting in the middle of a newly decorated room admiring our handiwork, he snorted as if outraged, "You lazy slobs! Do I have to do all the work?" Then with a wink to me and a couple of affectionate pats for the kids, he rushed off.

In theory, Emin Bey, the Prosecutor, was the one

responsible for recruiting civilian teachers, arranging the syllabus along Ministry guidelines, acquiring text-books and teaching aids. Mustafa was seething when he returned from meeting him. "He says two months! We'll have to start alone using anything we can find."

As a prisoner, I wasn't supposed to teach in the school, yet the next morning there I was – standing before a classroom packed with kids and adults. I couldn't attempt a formal lesson and was telling jokes when Mustafa appeared, lugging two suitcases. Sweating from his exertions, he lifted a case onto a desk top and, with a flourish, snapped it open. It was stuffed with textbooks, all bearing the stamps of Izmir libraries and schools. The kids squealed their delight. "Where did you get these?" I asked suspiciously. And Mustafa smiled serenely. "They were donated."

Over the next few days, Mustafa wheedled and blackmailed three other prisoners into volunteering as teachers: Orhan, Nahim and Fikret.

Orhan, a pokerfaced electrical engineer and wife-killer was to teach maths and science. Nahim, a poetry-spouting, hash-smoking journalist, took on literature and geography. Fikret, the ramrod-straight major con-victed of torture was allocated history and the Turkish constitution.

My speciality was English but I regularly stood in for Mustafa and taught literacy. I had learnt Turkish from scratch so it was easy to teach the basic links between the sounds of syllables and letters of the alphabet.

Mustafa had also recruited a sixth teacher, Jangir, to conduct Koran study classes. On the first day, Jangir heard Fikret start his history lesson and, in front of the class, immediately interrupted. Wagging his finger, he shouted, "No. Ataturk was an enemy of Islam. Why don't you tell them that?" There was a fierce argument between the two men. Jangir resigned on the spot.

The nearest we came to a formal opening was when Mustafa pinned a timetable to the wall. Our students gathered round the complicated chart and searched for their names. When someone showed the illiterate old men where their names were written, they always touched the place delicately before turning away. Many looked stunned as we gave them typewritten cards, the permits for them to leave their blocks and attend school. Locking up that evening, Mustafa briefly squeezed my arm. "That's it. Now it's a real school."

They were a mixed bunch, ever-changing because of releases, transfers and fluctuating enthusiasm, with a faithful core of regular attenders: fifty kids aged between ten and seventeen, forty common criminals who took middle and high school courses, and at least twenty *dadas*, old villagers who, after a lifetime of thumb-printing, wanted to sign their names. Political prisoners were barred from the school, by Ministry orders.

At first I had difficulty remembering all their names – they all had identical uniforms and shaven heads. I fell into the habit of using nicknames. Brooders, bullies, wisecrackers and know-alls. Big-city sophisticates, crafty village countrymen. Killers, muggers, rapists and thieves, they all had nicknames to match. Monster, my favourite teenager with a grotesquely scarred face. Whisky, with his big, red nose. Snake, the slit- eyed *Türkman*. Midget, Handsome, Four Eyes and German.

Discipline was never a problem. Many students came only out of boredom and curiosity but then developed an enthusiasm which would have been the envy of any conventional school. Often the lessons took off into free-ranging discussions on everything from cooking to global politics. Once I caught Mustafa in the corridor as he eavesdropped on a history lesson at the keyhole. He beamed at me impishly, "If Emin Bey heard this, he'd have a fit!"

Trouble was usually sparked off by the two school guards, Russian Soldier Ali and Spiderman Kemal.

Ali, thick-necked, built like a barrel with cropped blond hair and rimless glasses was a devout, five-prayer-sessions-a-day Muslim. I never once saw him smile. Kemal, a wispy Kurd with a high-pitched, nervous giggle, followed him like a yapping poodle.

Both men were hated by the prisoners. After a series of violent incidents, they rarely entered the prison blocks. The moment they appeared in the school, the atmosphere became rigid with fear. They never hid their scorn for its easygoing atmosphere and often terrorized the younger children with slaps and punches.

They barged into a literacy class during our second week. I tried to resume the lesson after the initial moment of silence. They waited by the door, studying the children. Suddenly, Ali swooped. He picked a cigarette butt up from underneath Monster's desk and caught the boy by the scruff of his neck. "You're from the juvenile block," he bellowed. "What are you doing with a cigarette?"

"It's not mine. I never smoke," Monster wailed. "Search me."

Ali screamed, "You're a lying bastard." Each word was accompanied by a vicious slap.

I tried to push between Ali and Monster. "It's mine," I quavered. "I smoked it before the lesson."

Ali clutched Monster's jacket collar and stared at me. "Show me your packet."

Hurriedly, I took out my cigarettes. Ali shook his head slowly. "No, it's not the same brand." Quite deliberately, he smashed Monster in the mouth. It was an immensely strong blow. I heard the sickening sound of Monster's teeth being torn from his gums and his agonized scream. Ali stared into my eyes as he continued to hold on to the sobbing bleeding youth.

The violence in his eyes mesmerized me. Abruptly, his point made, Ali released Monster and turned away, Kemal trailing behind.

I wanted to register a complaint with the Justice Ministry but Mustafa persuaded me not to. His face was white with anger. "The Prosecutor would use it as an excuse to close the school. No court would believe you. You're not even supposed to be here." He shrugged, "We've got to ignore them."

Our first indication that Emin Bey had relented was the arrival of several boxes of new textbooks, pencils and exercise books.

That same week, Mustafa thrust his nose around the door and pleaded dramatically. "Mesut is here. You're the only one who can talk with him. He's in Fikret's class."

It was an emergency. Mesut, the block chief of the four-hundred-odd Marxist militant prisoners, was a sworn enemy of Fikret, the ex-major who had interrogated and tortured many of his comrades. Anything was possible. I rushed into Fikret's class only to see Mesut sitting slouched on the back bench, sneering at Fikret, who was nervously carrying on with his lesson.

Mesut saw me and beckoned. "I hope you're not enjoying this place. We're closing it down." His voice was loud and threatening. "I never thought you'd become an arse-licker. What are you doing co-operating with these bastards? We can't allow the so-called history being taught here."

He stood abruptly and, clenching his fist so hard it trembled, he bellowed at Fikret, "And we don't like that Ataturk-loving swine teaching here."

The ex-major straightened and, eyes flashing, stood ready to confront Mesut. Nothing was more important to Fikret than his loyalty to Ataturk, the founding father of modern Turkey and its army.

I pushed Mesut down onto the bench and sat on the desk in front of him. He looked up at me with the weariness of an old con and said petulantly, "I've been here longer and know more about history than that bastard. Why can't I teach here?"

We ignored Fikret and the class and talked over the old days when we used to play chess together in the political block. "You're right," I agreed, "this school is a joke. I'm only here to pass the time. Your revolution was taking too long and I got fed up waiting."

"Sorry," he smiled at me. "It's a unanimous decision. We took a vote in the Marxist blocks. Unless you're closed by tomorrow there'll be trouble."

To soften Mesut's attitude and extract him from Fikret's classroom, I suggested, "Come and talk it over with Mustafa."

Mustafa was adept at treading the path between civil and military authority but the opposition of the politicals went beyond his knowledge and experience. He listened with a perplexed, polite smile as Mesut used revolutionary rhetoric to explain why the school had to close. He didn't try to argue. Later, after Mesut had left, I sat with him in the school kitchen.

"Don't worry," I assured him. "Mesut talks big but he's the only political allowed out of the blocks. By himself, what can he do?"

Months passed. The school became an integral part of the prison. The Prosecutor hired several civilians but none of them stayed long and we continued to work as temporary teachers.

When the Prosecutor came to the first literacy tests,

the school's future seemed guaranteed. He sat behind a large desk on the raised podium in front of the class. He wore a pink-flowered tie and a smart pin-striped suit. Miril Hanum, the enormous wardress from the women's block, sat beside him. She had exchanged her steel hair comb for a red ribbon. Behind them stood a row of head guards, unusually spruce and tidy.

The *dadas* fidgeted excitedly on the benches before the visitors. Mustafa stood in front of the Prosecutor, smiling encouragement and called, "Mohammed Aktuna."

Mumbling, *"Y'Allah, gidiyorum"*, I go with God, the first of the *dadas* shuffled to the front of the class and took a pen from Mustafa. I stood beside him with my arms folded and the *dada*, wearing his pocket watch, waistcoat and collarless shirt underneath a regulation blue jacket, slyly watched my finger. Whether it was bent, straight or slanted signified the shape of the first letter to his name.

Though just an ability to sign their names was being tested, the old men were only used to doing it on the blackboard. It required great effort and concentration to write on paper. As old Mohammed stepped up onto the podium and approached the desk, the entire class shouted support. With one last check on the shape of my finger, he nodded grimly to the Prosecutor, steeling himself for the ordeal.

Miril Hanum flicked through a pile of identity cards until she found the one bearing his photograph. She passed it to Prosecutor Emin Bey who pointed to the spot where the name had to be written. The *dada* then bent over the desk and laboriously penned his first official signature, thereby validating his prison identity card. Solemnly, he shook hands with the Prosecutor and guards before turning back to face the class. Holding up the signed card in triumph, he stood basking a moment in the wild applause before he returned to his place and sat proudly studying it.

Even Prosecutor Emin Bey smiled.

After that, although the Marxists included "Close the School. Prisoner Power" amongst the slogans they shouted out almost every evening, Mustafa, Fikret and I felt confident enough to turn their threats into a private joke. The more the Marxists yelled, the more popular we were with the Prosecutor.

Jangir, the Koran teacher who had only lasted a day, and the Islamic militant prisoners also caused trouble. They sent daily appeals and petitions to protest at the absence of Koran study classes, until finally the Prosecutor had to surrender. A religious teacher started to visit the prison weekly. But then the fundamentalists argued an hour a week was insufficient, that each day should begin with Koran study. Mostly old men, they hardly seemed a force to fear. To all of us, it was inconceivable that they would ever join forces with their sworn enemies, the Marxists.

I suspect it was Russian Soldier Ali who gave the fundamentalists the key to Mesut's block. They had obviously planned well ahead. It was a morning when the court was in session so very few soldiers were around. The fundamentalists opened the door of the Marxist block and unleashed a riot.

I was in the middle of an English class with half a dozen *lycée* candidates and some young children. I heard the thunder of running feet. A window shattered. Then Mesut, backed by twenty other militants and white-bearded fundamentalists, marched into the room. Mustafa appeared almost immediately and yelled to Mesut, "What's going on?" Mesut laughed, mocking us all. "I warned you." He went on with a sneer, "Don't worry. It's the school we're going to wreck. Stand clear, we don't want anyone to get hurt."

Two track-suited Marxist militants picked up the heavy wrought-iron stove and used it to smash the desks and benches. One carried a pot of black paint and, while his comrades collected all the books to make a bonfire in the courtyard, he painted *Eğitim ve Devrim Birlikte* – Education and Revolution Together – on the wall.

A well-spoken Marxist politely warned me to keep clear of glass splinters from the Ataturk portrait he was about to smash. I had to laugh.

In five minutes they had broken every desk, cupboard, bench and window in the school. Complete devastation.

First the Marxists and religious fundamentalists, then Mesut, shook hands with Mustafa and me and trooped back to their blocks. As Mesut touched my hand, I was speechless, unable to find words to express my shock and anger.

Seconds later the soldiers arrived, brandishing truncheons and swollen with protective padding. They looked disappointed there was no one to attack. Head Guard Jasim Baba trampled the glass fragments, kicked a broken desk in disgust and left to fetch the Prosecutor. Emin Bey didn't take long. Surveying the shambles, he glared at Mustafa as if he was to blame for the destruction. He left without saying a word, heading for the political's block. Head Guard Jasim Baba gave Mustafa a sympathetic smile before he led the soldiers after the Prosecutor.

Total silence. I sagged into a monkey crouch and hugged my knees. The kids looked stupified, paralysed by the extent of the damage. The school was a write-off.

Only one mind was alive. Mustafa's. He was standing motionless by the door. His eyes flickered round the room, as if making an inventory of the damage. Suddenly he clapped his hands. "OK. Let's get to work."

He had to be mad. Fikret began to speak for all of us. Couldn't he see the hopelessness of it all? Mustafa's gleaming eyes halted him mid-phrase.

Then Monster rolled his eyes, tapped his forehead meaningfully and started to heave debris into the courtyard. Somebody smiled, then laughed. Soon we were all emptying the classrooms in an orgy of activity. We worked yelling our frustration, cursing Marx, Jangir, and Reagan for luck, creating noise for the hell of it. The mess was cleared up in an hour.

Mustafa didn't pause for a second. Scribbling in a notebook, he said calmly, "So we start again. This time we'll need money. We've got to start quickly before the Prosecutor orders the school closed for good." Turning to me, he went on, "Try begging handouts from the rich blocks." And as an afterthought, "Take a couple of the smallest kids to make their hearts bleed."

It worked. We didn't have to beg. Miril Hanum arrived with an envelope of cash from the women's block only hours after the riot. There followed contributions from nearly every block in the jail. The biggest surprise was a donation from the Prosecutor. By evening we had more than 25,000 lire to rebuild the school.

Over the next days there were sometimes too many prisoners decorating and repairing for the job to be done efficiently. The chaos lasted a week. We still lacked textbooks and many students were forced to sit on the floor, but we were back in the teaching and learning business.

Two weeks before I was released from prison, the results of the middle and high school exams arrived. Thirty-three students had passed. A special ceremony was held to present the certificates.

The entire school was ushered into the auditorium and joined by Emin Bey, the Regional Prosecutor, several officials from the Justice Ministry, guards with their wives and a couple of important army officers. We all dutifully applauded the speeches until it was clear one name was missing from the roll-call of those being thanked and lauded. Mustafa.

Not that he seemed to mind. He sat beside me wearing his best suit, proud and delighted that so many of his students had qualified. When it was time to hand out the certificates, the Prosecutor stood alone on the stage searching his pockets for the list of students. He couldn't find it. Finally, embarrassed, he beckoned to Mustafa. Mustafa rose and walked onto the stage with his copy of the list.

Something burst. All the students, teachers and guards in the auditorium got to their feet. We clapped, stomped and cheered, creating a deafening uproar that went on and on. The mild, unassuming education director stood on the stage and blinked back tears.

Princess of the underworld

Aysha was more visible than any other woman in Buca Prison. She was an expert at lingering in the lawyers' interview room, remembering to recover a "forgotten" identity tag from a visiting booth, or creating scenes in the administration office. In prison, the sexes were totally separated by stringent precautions which prevented them from catching sight of each other. Yet the teenage Kurdish prostitute was a frequent if fleeting vision in our male-dominated institution.

Late one afternoon, I was returning a pile of ragged textbooks to the depot after a long day teaching in the prison school. I was tired. After two months of appeals, meetings and mental jousting, the Prosecutor had officially permitted English lessons. He nursed a deep mistrust for anything foreign or new, so I slaved at making my lessons a success.

Someone tapped me lightly on the shoulder. I turned to see Aysha, flushed, breathless and grinning. I gaped at her, frightened. She had actually touched me, something none of the erotic beauties who invaded my dreams had ever managed.

Not that Aysha could compare with those dream goddesses. Untidy locks of black hair hid most of her features. She wore a garish, yellow dress over her rather dumpy, small body. But none of my dream creatures had ever looked at me like that. Aysha's eyes locked me to the spot.

Miril Hanum, approaching at top speed, rescued me from that smitten condition. The head guard of the women's block was a cold shower to dampen the most ardent soul. She was an immense woman who hovered constantly behind Aysha like a brass- buttoned, peak-capped shadow.

Clawing for an escape from the spell, I heard Aysha say, "Danyel Effendi. Will you also teach the women English?"

Directing my attention more at Miril Hanum than at Aysha, I stuttered pompously, "Of course. Learning English would be helpful to begin a new life."

Aysha understood my predicament perfectly but she had no intention of letting me off the hook. Enunciating carefully, in a voice loud enough to be heard by every guard and official in the vicinity, she said cockily, "You're dead right, darling. If I could speak English I'd be able to pick up American sailors and earn much more money."

Whilst my morale soared on hearing that one word of endearment, Miril Hanum sped into action. Lips pursed, eyes glaring, she latched onto Aysha's arm and turned her away in one expert movement.

The petition from the women prisoners asking for English lessons was not turned down by the Prosecutor. Instead, in fine Turkish bureaucratic style, I was told to stop giving English lessons to the men.

Aysha was released after that two-month stint but was back again within weeks to lead Miril Hanum on the same chase.

With the English lessons abandoned, I spent more time in the foreigners' block but still caught the occasional glimpse of her. Invariably, she waved from a distance and I grinned and nodded a reply. I didn't keep track of her comings and goings but, since we were just two blocks down the corridor, I must have heard her welcomed in and cheered out half a dozen times. Her name often cropped up in prison conversations. She was also a favourite subject for gossip amongst the guards. Jarvid boasted of having once been her client.

In the beginning of May 1984, cries of "Aysha, Aysha" rang in the corridor. A short time later the guards duly reported. Aysha was back again. She had switched from prostitution to shoplifting and was also very pregnant.

Next day, I was on my way back from a consular visit when I saw her sitting in the administration office, tears of laughter in her eyes, holding her belly protectively.

Her status had changed. Perhaps the guards thought her pregnancy had defused her seductive appeal. Miril Hanum sat beside her with the usual stern expression but made no attempt to herd her back to the block.

By then I was a year short of release and one of the oldest lags in the prison, so no one stopped me from pausing to welcome her home. Patting her belly, she said proudly, "I've brought someone with me this time so I won't get lonely." I laughed, the guards laughed and even the corners of Miril Hanum's prim mouth twitched.

Aysha could be found in the administration office most evenings after six o'clock, as soon as the Governor and the civil administrators were off the premises. At least once a fortnight I used my old lag's prerogative to visit her. I wasn't the only one. Under one pretext or another, many prisoners just happened to call in at the office at the same time.

Seeing her was one thing, speaking with her was something quite different. Miril Hanum kept her trapped securely in a corner behind a wide desk and not a word could be exchanged without first obtaining permission. Miril Hanum's weakness was foreign cigarettes, preferably Marlboro. The full packet had to be placed conveniently on the desk from where it could be swept "accidentally" into her knitting bag. However, that only opened negotiations. Miril Hamun took her chaperone's responsibilities very seriously and was careful who talked with her ward.

The first criterion was lineage and standing in the criminal fraternity. Those guilty of crimes of passion and petty thieving stood no chance. Block chiefs, invariably gangsters, drug dealers or bank robbers were grudgingly admitted. Elderly white-collar fraudsters received Miril Hanum's broadest come-hither smiles. Next, she took account of cleanliness, dress and general demeanour. More than one eminent Mafia chief was turned away for having a five o'clock shadow or dirty fingernails. Aysha, apparently fascinated by all men, was never consulted, but whether the suitor was a bald old crock or a virile, handsome youth, her sunny disposition never changed.

A good number of the words I shared with Aysha touched on her health. Back at the block, the other foreign prisoners quizzed me thoroughly on the subject. They put her down for being a prostitute who didn't even know who her child's father was, but, despite themselves, they still cared about her.

Anything was a break from the soul-destroying boredom of prison. At that time, there was a daily TV programme of keep-fit exercises for pregnant women. Suddenly, it had a regular male audience. In everyone's mind, Aysha was transformed into the elastic-limbed blonde model they saw cavorting across the screen. The men watched the programme, urging aloud, "That's it Aysha. You're doing fine." Afterwards, they used to sit around gossiping, obsessed with the dangers of child-birth.

The prison doctor found he had to answer searching questions about pregnancy and birth, posed by the gruffest of men.

A month before Aysha's child was due, the doctor casually revealed to one inquisitive prisoner that, unless there were complications, Aysha would not be sent to hospital. The news was all over the prison in minutes. Guards and prisoners alike growled, "Why? Isn't she good enough for hospital care?" A deputation of block chiefs demanded to see the Prosecutor. The scribe of each block wrote long-winded moralistic letters to newspapers. Some prisoners threatened to riot.

Aysha defused our crisis. She laughed when old Kurt Kemal advised her, on behalf of us all, to have the baby in hospital. "Why should I? I trust the doctor. All my friends are here." Patting the Kurdish block chief's hand, she added, "Don't worry. This is my home."

The old block chief did worry and spoke of his doubts to everybody he met. An hour later, a large group of the left-wing politicals and ageing Islamic fundamentalists marched down the corridor to the administration office, shouting the slogan, "No innocent babes behind bars."

Head Guards Ismail and Jasim Baba shrugged. "She's free to do what she likes. We can't order her to go to hospital."

The politicals and fundamentalists returned to their blocks to draft petitions and appeals. Still angry, they sent a delegation to all the blocks in the prison to explain their views.

"The child will be stigmatized. We have a social obligation to protect it," said Mesut, the Marxist chief. "It is written in the Koran. A child should not be stained with the sins of elders," growled Jangir, the fundamentalist leader.

Everybody had a view to express. Most agreed with Mesut and Jangir. Then Claudio, a young Italian lifer, asked Gemal thoughtfully, "What about Aysha? Doesn't she have any say in it?" Sayed Ali, overhearing as he poured tea, was stunned. "He's right. Who are we to interfere?"

Sayed Ali was more talkative than usual selling tea that evening and, overnight, the mood of the foreign prisoners changed. Aysha suddenly became a heroine. Maybe her decision to have a jailhouse birth was rooted in commonsense and comfort considerations. However, we saw it as proof of her courage and loyalty.

"Yes," the bemused doctor assured, "Aysha does the fitness exercises shown on television. She's in the best of health." Frowning, men returned to their blocks and began to work. Knitters clicked. A carpenter made an elaborate cradle out of spent matches. The patch-sewer raided his cache to create a special quilt. Khomeyon, a soft-eyed sentimental Iranian, embroidered sheets with delicate, colourful designs from the *Rubaiyat* of Omar Khayyam.

Tension was fuelled by the birth of a baby to the television model. Yes, it was cute and bawled like an auctioneer, but it wasn't Aysha's. We quickly resolved the squabbles which erupted over nothing; it was improper to quarrel at such a time

And one morning, when we were standing in line waiting for the dawn count, Head Guard Jasim Baba substituted the usual "Good morning" bellow with an exultant, "It's a girl!"

All the men returned to their cells looking relieved and despatched their presents to Aysha.

Six weeks passed with no sight of Aysha or her

baby. We only had the doctor's exasperated reassurance, "They're both fine!" Then, one Saturday morning, Zeki and I were ordered to the administration office. Aysha had requested our company. Pagan Ali muttered cynically, "Take your wallets. It's Aysha's payday."

Miril Hanum was tight-lipped. Aysha was trapped in the usual corner, smiling serenely and clutching her baby, who was wrapped in a magnificent multi-coloured quilt. Guards lined the walls and stood stiffly to attention as we joined a line of twenty zoot-suited, glossy-shoed prisoners. Altogether, forty men, half of them puffing nervously on cigarettes, two women and a baby were crammed into a tiny, unventilated office in mid July.

Sweat poured and smoke billowed as we began the formalities of shaking every hand in the office. Suddenly, Miril Hanum, the realist, shouted, "Open the door, the baby's baking. Aysha wants to call her *Gümüsh*. Let's get on with it."

Each of us in turn, including the guards, gravely took the squirming, crying bundle from Aysha, tucked bank notes beneath her wrap and whispered, "*Gümüsh*" – Silver – into a tiny ear.

I held her for only a second. Her smell and moist skin shocked me. My well-rehearsed congratulatory phrase emerged as an incoherent croak. I almost threw Gümüsh back into Aysha's waiting arms. The two women exchanged knowing looks and I shot out of the office to gulp down some prison air.

In the corridor, Mesut and Jangir crouched outside the tea shop. To return to the foreigners' block, I had to pass them.

Jangir held out a glass of tea and fixed me with his usual fanatical stare, "*Salaam alaykum*."

I accepted the glass and squatted beside them.

57

"She doesn't stand a chance. She'd be better off dead," Mesut sneered.

"The baby should go to an orphanage," Jangir pontificated. "That whore has no right to keep it."

"The orphanage is more squalid than the prison," I said, angered. "She'd be just one more mouth to feed. Here, at least she gets to stay with Aysha. She's got a hundred doting aunts and three thousand uncles. She's like a princess of the underworld."

Mesut

I remember Mesut from his first spell in Izmir Prison which, considering the number of young politicals I met behind bars, is quite astonishing. That time, he only served a four-month sentence for gun possession but he stood out as a sharp dresser, more relaxed and cheerful than his intense, studious comrades. He was also an occasional opponent in our five-a-side soccer matches, foreigners against the politicals.

Despite his youth, Mesut was respected for his experience and contacts amongst the left-wing militant organizations. He was talked about in the prison.

As an eighteen-year-old unemployed high school graduate, Mesut, like thousands of his contemporaries, had become involved in the political turmoil of those years.

Gangs of armed youths roamed Istanbul, stopping strangers in the street to ask, "Are you Right or Left?" The wrong answer often meant a bullet in the head; an evasive answer, a bullet in the knee. Mesut had been a fund collector for a small Marxist faction. Standing at street corners, one hand clutching a gun hidden in his anorak pocket, he sold left-wing tracts at inflated prices.

In 1977, Mesut escaped from Bayrampasha Prison, the main high-security jail in Istanbul where he had been awaiting trial for membership of an illegal political organization. His escape was a mixture of chance and quick wits. Dev Yol – Path to Revolution – the most powerful Marxist organization in Turkey, had worked out a scheme to free two Palestinian guerrillas. Mesut latched onto the Palestinians at the crucial moment and followed them to freedom through a dismantled inspection hatch. At first, many prisoners condemned Mesut for jeopardizing the escape but, as everything went well, it made his name as a smart operator.

From Istanbul, equipped by Dev Yol with false identity papers, he was directed to a safe-house in Izmir, a west-coast holiday resort. During the day the house was a printing works and electronic repair shop. At night it became the meeting place for a band of armchair revolutionaries.

From the beginning, Mesut was an object of awe to his hosts. He was a big-city, street-wise cowboy with an introduction from the top theoreticians of Dev Yol. Hussein, the sad-faced erudite elder of the Izmir militants, later explained, "We thought they sent him to lead us into the streets. He made us come alive."

Mesut was experienced. He'd been in street battles, strikes and demonstrations and knew about weapons. He fitted their image of a proletarian fighter, tall and broad with wide slavonic features and trust-inspiring eyes. He was code-named "Fridge" because he stayed cool in dire situations.

Hussein often recalled the night a main street was blocked with blazing tractor tyres. "We all ran. Only Mesut stayed behind to spray the firemen with bullets."

Mesut's most active year was 1980. Many organizations combined to stage a nationwide rehearsal for the revolution. He was the dynamo of the Izmir action. When he reappeared behind bars in 1981, he was a grown man facing a serious charge – the murder of a police-informer.

Mesut was held in E7, a mixed block of common prisoners and left-wing politicals. E7's courtyard was shared with foreign prisoners. Turgut, a muddle-headed university lecturer, officially represented the block but Mesut was the *de facto* chief. Everybody knew it was only a question of time before he was transferred to Death Row. That alone made him someone the men looked up to and respected.

The army had been in control of the jail since the 1980 military coup. The civilian guards lounged in the corridors, deprived of the authority even to handle a door key. Jasim Baba, a guard with twenty years experience, was truncheon-whipped by two teenage soldiers. His crime had been to have a whispered conversation with me through a slit in the door.

Mesut's block became a hotbed of insurrection, its inmates defiant and united. Around one hundred and fifty men scorned the soldiers and goaded them until they reacted. Fights happened daily until the prison was kept permanently locked-down. Even visits were cancelled. Every time Mesut's block door had to be opened to deliver food or collect rubbish, prisoners spilled out into the corridors and the soldiers beat them back inside the block.

Mesut inspired much of the provocation. He had the credibility to enthuse common prisoners. Unlike Turgut, Mesut talked the slang of the streets. Throughout the prison, because of Mesut and others like him, the military's attempt to dilute the strength of the politicals by mixing them with common criminals backfired badly.

Mesut also understood the psychology of the soldiers and how to undermine their confidence in the officers. Although many of his comrades suffered truncheon

blows, when Mesut confronted the soldiers, they instinctively held back. He was destined for execution and had
nothing to lose but they also respected him. Other difficult political prisoners were weeded out and transferred
to military jails but Mesut was the prime suspect in an
important trial and had to remain in Izmir.

I spent a lot of time in E7, playing football or chess
and teaching English. As Turkish books, newspapers and
magazines were strictly censored, any foreign publica-
tions on politics or Turkey that I brought along were
highly prized. Mesut wasn't easy to befriend. Sometimes
he was moody, lying on his bunk and glowering at the
bars. Often his voice was disturbingly loud and strident.
I put it down to the pressures of leadership but I always
felt attracted by his courage, confidence and charisma.
His sense of loyalty to his cause and to his comrades
impressed me.

Mesut's trial took nine months. On the day of the
verdict, he was taken to Death Row for the long wait
until his execution.

Following Mesut's departure from E7, the army separated common and political prisoners. Boldly asserting
that it would foster brotherhood behind bars, they
crammed right- and left-wing politicals together into the
same dormitories for a whole year. It led to a number of
terrible fights. When the political prisoners maimed or
killed each other, the soldiers laughed.

Mesut spent the year cooped up in a cell with
an infamous right-wing assassin. Under the military,
prisoners awaiting execution received only food; letters,
visits, newspapers, everything was forbidden. The cell
had no light, windows or bunks and was over-run with
rats and cockroaches. The two men slept on the floor and
had to huddle together under a single blanket to survive
the winter.

The hangman was kept busy throughout 1982 but Mesut's execution was delayed by an appeal. Against all our expectations, the Appeal Court commuted his sentence. From having no future at all, Mesut suddenly faced a lifetime behind bars.

When I met him in the administration office the following summer, Mesut appeared unchanged. He was standing between two soldiers, pounding on a desk, shouting, "I'm a political prisoner. Nobody can make me wear a uniform." Seeing me, he was suddenly all smiles and charm. He hugged my shoulders and drew me into a corner. A soldier snatched at my arm to hustle me past and Mesut pushed him back, warning, "Don't touch him. He's under my protection." No one answered. I was puzzled by the tolerance shown him.

Later that year, when the reorganized civilian administrators took back control of the prison, they still turned a blind eye to Mesut's provocations. Not only did he have a free run of the prison, he was the only inmate I met in twelve years to receive proper dental care.

For a time, the velvet glove treatment mellowed his belligerence. He became more of a jailhouse negotiator, knowing and demanding his rights. Then more political prisoners arrived. Again there were fights and hunger-strikes. Mesut was always their strong and courageous leader. Only after he led the riot which destroyed the prison school did I lose my admiration for him.

I had worked hard to open the school and its destruction infuriated me. Like virtually all the common prisoners, I had no patience or sympathy left for the extremists. And I was angry about the new "penitents" legislation which had just been introduced. This law, modelled on an Italian experiment, was designed to encourage terrorists in prison to inform on comrades still outside. It offered them a variety of rewards including total amnesty, depending on the prisoner's co-operation and a public declaration of penitence. The law generated so much controversy that it took a year to put into operation.

Out of the seven hundred political prisoners in Izmir, only sixteen applied to participate in the penitents' scheme. For security reasons, the informers were isolated. The children in the block opposite ours were moved and the informers took their place. The majority of the informers were young men charged with comparatively mild offences.

Mesut ridiculed them. Standing in the corridor outside the foreigners' block, he laughed, "The fools. For a few names to save a few years, they're dead men as soon as they step out of jail."

Four days later, Mesut asked to turn informer and was accepted. Supposedly to keep it secret, he was transferred at three o'clock in the morning. In reality, the administration used the silence of the night to emphasize a victory. Literally hundreds of soldiers in full battle-gear woke the whole prison as they marched to take up positions on either side of the mile-long corridor and stood to attention like a guard of honour as Mesut strode between them. Through inspection hatches and slits, we watched with unbelieving eyes. From the political blocks came deafening waves of the chant, "Death to traitors", interspersed with eerie silences.

After I recovered from the shock of seeing him turn informer, I had to decide how to treat him. Like the other foreigners, I received a note from the politicals asking me to ignore the informers, especially Mesut. To show our solidarity, we wanted to comply but it wasn't so simple. Mesut may have been one of the most important informers in Turkey but he was also an old mate.

The administration tried their best to reduce contact

between foreigners and informers by regulating our access to the shared courtyard. For half the day it was opened to the informers. Then they were locked back in their block and until evening it was opened to us. The bars over the windows and courtyard gates prevented us from having physical contact but conversation was easy.

Mesut was always waiting. Whenever I stepped into the courtyard, he called to me. His candour was startling. If he had been self-righteous or over-regretful, there would have been something tangible to dislike. But he claimed he still admired his old comrades' tenacity and that he had betrayed them reluctantly. "I'm still a Marxist," he explained earnestly, "but living with that fascist psychopath on Death Row started me thinking."

Shame-faced, he confided, "I don't think I'm strong enough to spend my whole life in jail." I couldn't hate him. When he apologized for wrecking the school, his sincerity overcame my doubts and contempt.

From his first day with the informers, Mesut once again took command. He decided all the practical arrangements and delegated reponsibilities in the block. His domineering and threatening attitude challenged fellow prisoners to dispute his authority. The informers, awed by his reputation and tough physique, submitted meekly.

Every morning he was taken to be interrogated by the political police. After a fortnight, they intensified his questioning and he spent week-long periods in the security police headquarters. He returned to the block subdued, unable or unwilling to speak.

Three months passed and the interrogation calls became less frequent. Mesut now stood for hours by the window, smiling invitingly at foreigners exercising in the courtyard. Outwardly, he seemed relaxed but there

65

was an emptiness in his conversation when I went over to speak to him. If I brought up any topic of substance, he became tongue-tied and hesitant.

One day, I was standing in the courtyard by Mesut's block with Albino, another British prisoner. We were chatting with Engin, the youngest informer. As we leaned on the window-ledge, Mesut edged closer, his expression lost and forlorn. His humility suddenly made me feel sick. Abruptly, I broke off the conversation with Engin and made a thin excuse to slip away. Albino held onto my arm and glared at Mesut. "Why don't you go somewhere and die? You're no good to anybody. They've cut off your balls and you're not pretty enough to be a fag."

Mesut lunged forward, then howled like an animal when Albino stepped out of reach. He bellowed threats and curses so loudly that guards and prisoners came rushing. No one attempted to pacify him. For several minutes everybody stood motionless, watching Mesut scream and strain at the bars.

Winter was severe that year and for two months the courtyard between the two blocks was hardly used. From time to time, newspaper articles reminded us of Mesut's existence by naming him as the star state witness in various trials. Altogether, more than a hundred people were convicted on his testimony. Three ex-comrades were sentenced to death, a former girlfriend received life imprisonment. All the politicals I spoke with swore much of his evidence was false.

Spring arrived, the weather improved and Mesut emerged from his block to play soccer in the courtyard with the other informers. I was struck by his odd movements. They were jerky, unco-ordinated, a far cry from his former athletic fluidity. When challenged, he surrendered the ball to his opponent rather than risk physical contact. As the player streaked away with the ball, Mesut stopped dead in his tracks, grimaced and muttered insults.

At the end of April, there was a security lapse. Two politicals stabbed Mesut in the lawyers' office. From hospital Mesut accused the Prison Governor of incompetence and nine informers of withholding information. The political police took his statements seriously and the Governor was demoted. The informers named by Mesut were excluded from the penitents' amnesty and sent back to normal blocks. One was later murdered by political prisoners.

Mesut spent two months in the hospital. When he returned to the informers' block, there were only six men left. It was just after noon and I was jogging round the courtyard when he called me over to a window. He was thin and his eyes blazed hostility. "You foreigners should watch out. I'm the most powerful man in this jail now," he boasted. "I even got rid of the Governor."

The six remaining informers tolerated Mesut for only a few days. At their own request, they were shifted to punishment cells. The long-term foreign prisoners had a meeting and voted to sever all contact with him. From that day on, whenever Mesut called to a foreigner, he was ignored. He was completely alone in the forty-man capacity block.

Months passed. Fearful of his enemies, shunned by the foreigners, Mesut was a shadowy, soliloquizing figure lurking behind dirt-encrusted windows.

Early one morning, in the spring of 1986, I saw him half-heartedly exercising in the courtyard. As soon as he realized he was being watched from a window, he retreated back into his block. That day, Tarik, a newly arrived Lebanese prisoner, was seen talking to him at the window. Zeki, an Egyptian lifer, didn't stop to listen to any excuses. He dragged Tarik away by the back of his shirt and hurled him across the courtyard, shouting, "Keep away from that snake."

Mesut stood at the window, glowering.

After that, although we rarely saw him, we detested him. Our revulsion increased after a newspaper article reported that his co-operation might be rewarded with a total amnesty. Foreigners sometimes shouted taunts at him but it was an accident when our soccer ball snapped the washing line Mesut had strung between two windows of his block. His newly-washed clothes fell to the ground but we went on with our soccer game and kicked them around. By the time Mesut came to the window to ask for his clothes back, they were ripped and muddied. Yorgo, the Greek, apologized as he gathered up the filthy rags. When Mesut stretched out his arm to take them, Yorgo laughed and hurled the clothes in his face.

It was not only the foreigners and politicals that despised Mesut. Throughout the prison his name had come to symbolize treachery. Early one morning, Ali Amja stopped his mobile shop outside Mesut's block. Ali Amja had worked the shop for ten years and was a barometer of prison attitudes. When Mesut came out to buy milk, Ali Amja pushed him so roughly that he dropped and broke open his cartons. Mesut raged. Ali refused to replace them and smiled, "Go tell the cops."

Mesut tried to hit back. At seven o'clock one morning he turned the TV on full volume, blasting our entire block awake with the Turkish national anthem. When Head Guard Ismail came we heard Mesut shout, "I'm proud of our anthem. What's wrong with that?" Ismail took our side and threatened to confiscate Mesut's TV.

On another occasion Mesut shouted from his window to an army officer during a search, "The foreigners have got wine hidden in the drain sumps."

We cursed Mesut and watched the soldiers carry away our hooch made from fermented potatoes and rice. That night, Jasim Baba sneaked half the bottles back and joined our impromptu drinking party. At three o'clock in the morning, Zeki hollered drunkenly until Mesut appeared at a window. Hooting triumph, Zeki threw an empty wine bottle across the courtyard. It smashed on the bars before Mesut's face and showered him with splinters.

I don't know what triggered the final explosion. One summer morning, when Mesut was out in the courtyard, he suddenly darted to a window of our block and screamed at a foreigner. We could all hear his crescendo of taunts and curses as he plunged his fists through every window within reach.

The foreigners ran to the windows to see him. We scrambled and shoved for a better view.

He stood alone in the middle of the courtyard, waving hands which were by then no more than lumps of bloody, torn flesh. His eyes stared maniacally, bulging and swivelling from side to side. He roared incomprehensibly. Saliva foamed from his mouth. His face was so convulsed, his jaw appeared dislocated and adrift.

"Now your throat," Niko screamed. "Slit your throat." And we all laughed until our sides ached.

Pagan Ali

The old man protectively clasped hands to his beard and pleaded passionately with the lieutenant, "Why cut it? I'm just one drop in a flood." Adnan smiled, "*Hoja*, I'm just following orders. Complain to General Evren."

The man sat down on the stool, softly reciting a Koranic passage, and the experienced soldier sheared off the beard in four swift sweeps. "See. Doesn't he look better?" the young lieutenant grinned at me.

"That beard was important to him," I sighed as the old man shuffled miserably away.

"Perhaps, but there are too many like him," Adnan slumped in his chair and sounded tired. "The east is crawling with them. They plod from village to village with their beards and Korans. The peasants feed them because they all look like Ayatollah Khomeini."

I nodded. The surge of Muslim fundamentalism sweeping the Islamic world made me feel insecure. I kept my fears in check by staying abreast of the news and developments.

Turkey's eastern neighbour, Iran, pumped out hours of Turkish-language radio broadcasts preaching Islamic revolution. Newspapers daily reported the arrests of unofficial *hojalar* who had encouraged draft-dodging or non-payment of taxes. Almost every night, the television news showed General Evren, the head of the military

71

government. I found his bellicose speeches far from reassuring.

However, in the foreigners' wing of Izmir prison, all that usually seemed very distant and unimportant. The majority of us were Muslim but we didn't worry about religion.

Weeks before the month-long fast of Ramazan, Ali confided to me nervously, "This year will be bad. Half the block is planning to fast." Ali was Islamophobic. Despite being the son of a well-known Egyptian religious scholar, he had been nick-named "Pagan" as soon as he started his life sentence. It was such a long-standing joke that Ali had once accidentally signed the nickname on an official document applying for a prison transfer.

My decade-old friendship with him was based on our shared disdain for all religions. Since a Turkish prison is no place to scorn Allah, we had developed a whispered dialogue of irreligious witticisms over the years. By joining the European prisoners, Ali used to avoid the monthly Mevlut night, when the television screened only special prayer services. While most of his Arab friends squeezed into a ground-floor cell to conduct prayer meetings, Ali came upstairs with us, to swig hooch, holler pop songs and joke about Islamic rituals. Ali clearly revelled in our blasphemous chatter.

Just as Ali had predicted, an unprecedented number of foreign prisoners signed the list showing they intended to fast. The list was given to the kitchen manager who would have to provide a meal each night for up to a thousand prisoners scattered throughout thirty blocks.

Europeans only had to suffer sleepless nights. Lapsed Muslims like Pagan Ali became the focus of the fasters' Islamic zeal.

Only rehabilitated junkies could ever rival their self-righteousness. Towards evening, when their nicotine cravings and hunger pangs increased, the fasters resorted to fervent prayers and the distraction of religious discussions.

Ali squatted in my cell and grumbled, "This is the worst hour. They all think I could be their ticket to paradise." He flashed his dark brown eyes indignantly. "Just because my father is a mullah, they think I must have some good in me. I'll have to kill somebody to prove I'm all bad."

I laughed. Ali was a wispy featherweight who jumped each time a cell gate slammed.

His main adversary was Gemal, an immense, muscular lifer with black staring eyes blazing from under a neolithic brow. His brutish appearance was deceptive. Gemal had a sharp, intelligent mind and an eloquent, persuasive tongue. As a long-time friend of Ali, he seemed to think the salvaging of Ali's soul was his personal duty. He was always good-natured about it, joking around the block, "Has anybody seen Pagan Ali? I've got to save him from himself before he goes free."

Ali spent so much time with me and the other Europeans that Gemal was forced to put up with our cynicism whenever he tried to draw Ali into religious debates. The moment Allah was mentioned, Ali would immediately switch from Arabic to Turkish, the *lingua franca* of the block. Gemal's position was further weakened by my knowledge of his past. Ten years earlier he had been my drug-bingeing partner when we were both looking desperately at the wrong end of life sentences. It made it difficult for him to moralize convincingly.

Gemal was good humoured but tenacious. Inevitably, our daily discussions, lying on cushions in a shaded corner of the courtyard, began to attract listeners. Most of the audience were villagers, simple men from the Syrian hills and Nile delta who had never heard anyone criticize Islam.

It was mid summer. Listening to Gemal Hoja explaining about the Prophet Mohammed to the "heathens" was a good way to pass the hottest hours of the day. Provocatively, we accused Islam of fostering intolerance and hypocritical attitudes. Udo, the German radical, labelled it a tool for oppressing the poor in bankrupt countries. Very few of our listeners understood abstract argument. It was Claudio, the gentle Italian hippy, who most upset them when he stuttered nervously, "There's no real love or compassion in Muslim countries." Our audience lapsed into a long, uncomfortable silence.

During the second week of Ramazan, Mustafa and Kemal decided to break off the fast. Kemal was a short-sentence Tunisian so nobody really cared. But Mustafa was a lifer from Cairo and a close friend of Gemal. The two men claimed the fast was making them ill. Both were young and seemingly healthy.

Our innuendos about the two abstainers were unsubtle. "Maybe Allah is asking too much," Yorgo baited Gemal.

"He who closeth his heart to Allah shall never obtain tranquillity," Gemal replied, with a patient smile.

Nico, the Spaniard whose back was decorated with a large tattoo depicting Christ on the cross, waved his bible. "Verily, I say unto you, in my Father's house there are many mansions." Grinning, digging his finger in Gemal's ribs, he went on, "Don't take it to heart, Gemal. Jesus will forgive you."

Gemal increased the prayer meetings to twice a day although fewer men attended. We continued to stretch out in the shade of the high prison wall. When Gemal refused to join us, Ali said, gratefully, "He's surrendered. I'm off the hook for another year." I wasn't so hopeful.

The atmosphere was too tense, something was brewing.

Finally Sheker Bayram, the festival signifying the end of Ramazan, arrived. Sheker Bayram also stood for brotherhood, forgiveness and the healing of enmities. All the prisoners dressed in their best clothes and stood in line to shake hands with the commander as he toured the blocks distributing sweets and cigarettes.

It was three o'clock in the morning when the cries woke me. They had an eerie, hysterical ring and grew louder and louder.

"*Allahu Akbar!*"

Even in my sleep-fogged state, I recognized the traditional Muslim call to prayers. But the cries were too strident to be the usual muted tape-recording broadcast from the prison minaret. Then I heard familiar grumbled curses as men climbed sluggishly from their bunks.

With the other pyjama-clad men, I stumbled bleary-eyed and apprehensive out into the corridor. We tracked the cries to the lower floor of the block and saw Gemal.

It was a startling, disturbing vision. Gemal, wearing a white *jalabar* and head-scarf, was standing on a window-ledge at the end of the corridor, holding the window bars, high above the men squeezed into the corridor. He was staring up into the white light of a huge full moon, his free hand cupped round his mouth to amplify the cry, "*Allahu Akbar!*" The cries, the moon, Gemal's messianic appearance – I stood and gaped.

The thick iron door leading to the access corridor screeched open and ten truncheon-wielding soldiers marched into the block. Behind them strolled Adnan, one hand on his pistol.

Gemal turned to face his audience, his voice deep and compelling. "The Prophet Mohammed has visited me in a dream," he cried in peasant Turkish. "He has chosen me to rid this place of heathens."

Pagan Ali crept up beside me, his eyes wide with astonishment. "He's flipped. Do something or they'll cart him off to the mad-house."

The soldiers made no move. Shocked and frightened, they pocketed their truncheons and waited for Adnan's orders. Adnan pushed through the crowd of prisoners and stood beneath Gemal. "Go on," Ali poked my ribs. "You're the block chief. Don't let Adnan take him away."

I went and stood beside Adnan. "Come down Gemal," Adnan called. "You can tell everybody about it in the morning." Gemal's firmness had a clear, charismatic authority. "I must not fail Allah. I must obey him."

Suddenly, he pointed an accusing finger at me and shouted, "You are the pagan spawn of the devil. I won't let you drag my brothers to hell."

"You tell him Gemal," Nico laughed. "Then we can get back to bed." I smiled up at Gemal but couldn't be bothered to argue and returned to my bunk.

The next morning, Ali described how Gemal had stood on the window-ledge until dawn, talking with Adnan and a large number of prisoners. He had demanded that Adnan should transfer me to another block and many of those listening had agreed. "You're lucky to be alive. Gemal wanted to slit your throat," Ali said with a grin. "Only Adnan and the first muezzin saved you."

A phoney truce reigned for a day. Ali reassured me that there was nothing to worry about, that the ill-feelings would fade and be forgotten. To be on the safe side, I kept to my cell.

On the second night after Gemal's outburst, I was woken by Ali's terrified shouts for help and ran downstairs to his cell. I was too late. Pagan Ali lay sprawled on the ground, blood streaming from his nose,

Gemal standing over him, screaming abuse in Arabic and kicking him viciously in the ribs.

The soldiers and Adnan, who had been expecting trouble, burst through the lower corridor access door and overpowered Gemal, pinning him to the wall. "He's a Muslim," Gemal shouted. "Either he prays with us or to save his soul, I swear I'll kill him."

My control snapped, I lunged forwards but Adnan held my shoulder. "Until you all learn to live peacefully, this block will be split," he calmly ordered. "Anybody who wants to live with Gemal stays downstairs. Anyone who doesn't will sleep upstairs. The gate between you will be locked."

Ali, Mustafa and a few other prisoners collected belongings and there and then moved to upstairs cells. Gemal glowered but said nothing. The gate separating the floors was locked and, except for snores, the block became quiet.

Ali was too nervous to sleep, so Adnan and I sat drinking tea with him. Smiling with relief, I congratulated the lieutenant. "It might work for a while."

It was 5 a.m. The sky lightened and the muezzin began the dawn call to prayers. The hypnotic tones sounded unusually clear. We averted our eyes and listened.

As Adnan got up to leave, I asked, "What if the old man with the beard was right? You can't dam a flood by closing prison doors."

"There's no flood to dam," Adnan smiled, leaning against the door-post. "True believers aren't drops of water."

77

Erim and Abdullah

"What a punk. A nobody," the plump guard shouted.

The slim, athletic young man reddened with indignation as he stepped over the threshold into the reception area. Immediately, the guard slammed the enormous steel door shut, locking him inside Istanbul's infamous Bayrampasha prison, named the Feast of the Lord.

Another guard, older and almost bald, with four red stripes on his jacket cuff, emerged from the office and walked towards the young man. He eased himself into a hard chair with a rheumatic wince. In a slow, impersonal voice he read from a dossier which contained a single sheet of paper.

"Family name – Nihat. Father's name – Edwan. First name – Erim. Age – nineteen. No previous convictions or arrests. Charges – drunk and disorderly conduct, assault on a police officer." He looked up and barked, "Is that right?"

Erim pulled at his bloodstained t-shirt and nodded, "Yes, sir."

The guard coldly recited his habitual warning. "I'm the top man here. You'll call me Salih Effendi. If you're smart, you'll do what I tell you." Turning to his companion, "You're right. He's a nobody. Throw him in the cage with the loonies. We'll process tomorrow."

The plump guard took Erim's arm and led him to a

barred cage on the other side of the hall, opposite the reception office. Unlocking the barred door, he pushed Erim inside.

Six gaunt, silent men sat on their haunches at the back of the cage. They looked at Erim with vacant, expressionless eyes. Erim began to smile at them, then gagged on the stench of their ragged, urine-soaked clothes.

A cheerful voice beside him said, "Ignore them. They're waiting to go to the nuthouse. Harmless. The lucky swine are doped to the eyeballs."

Erim turned. The speaker was a thin young man in tight jeans, with a sharp, pointed face and sunken, cunning eyes. He offered Erim his hand. "My name's Villi but everybody calls me Devil. I'm a regular here."

The two men crouched close to the bars and talked compulsively as if to create an island of sanity in the cage.

Erim covered his face with his hands. "I was so drunk. I can't remember hitting the cop. They announced the exam results in the morning and we celebrated all day. Look at me! One of the cops kicked me in the face. My jeans are stiff with blood. The bastards wouldn't even let me pick up fresh clothes."

Villi snorted. "You college kids. You're supposed to be smart. At least I'm here for something that counts," he grinned proudly. "I broke into a chemist. Nearly got away with ten boxes of tranqs."

Late that evening, the plump guard opened the main door of the reception area for a second time, letting in a cleansing draught of fresh air.

The man who entered wore a sleek camel-hair coat. He waited calmly in the centre of the hall as the guard ran into the reception office crying, "Salih. Wake up." Head Guard Salih came out sleepily rubbing his eyes, saw who had arrived and rushed back into the office to fetch a chair. The two guards sat talking with the newcomer who distributed American cigarettes, lighting them with a chunky, gold lighter. Fawning and respectful, the guards thanked him.

The newcomer nodded distastefully at the cage. "You collecting pigs in there, Salih?"

"Yeah. Crazies and kids. It's been quite a night," the guard laughed.

After they had drunk tea, Salih led the man away, almost bowing as he showed him through a small gate leading out into the prison complex.

"Was that the prison director?" Erim asked his new friend.

"That's Abdullah Chitin. He's dangerous," Villi warned. "Keep out of his way. He's big time in the rackets."

"Why aren't we taken straight into the prison like him?" Erim asked angrily.

"We're not Abdullah," Villi laughed, "If you want to get out of here alive, never ask questions like that. Just do everything they tell you."

The next morning, Erim and Villi were taken upstairs and left alone, handcuffed to a radiator at the end of a wide corridor. Administration offices led off on either side. As the morning progressed, clerks, secretaries and visitors busily criss-crossed the corridor, staring with horrified fascination every time they passed the handcuffed men.

Villi talked avidly, blind to their humiliating gaze. Erim crouched beside him, turning his back to the corridor, and immersed himself in Villi's tales of Istanbul's hoodlums and racketeeers.

A trustee prisoner in a blue uniform approached holding a pair of hair-clippers. "Don't pay him," Villi warned Erim. "That bastard expects money for shaving your head. His kind always rip off us cons."

As the clippers sheared away his hair down to the scalp, Erim caught the eyes of a woman watching him intently. He looked away, embarrassed.

It was early afternoon before Erim and Villi were handcuffed together and taken into an office to be finger-printed and photographed. Erim remembered Villi's advice and submitted without protest as the guard unlocked the cuffs with bad-tempered haste, cursing and pushing them through the procedures. Filthy, ragged, cotton uniforms were thrust into their hands. Erim followed Villi's example and pulled the uniform on over his own clothes. "You got to be smart. Only suckers hand over their civvies," Villi winked.

They spent two more hours chained to the radiator so it was evening when they were finally shoved, handcuffed together, though an iron door into a small, glass-walled office. The guard lolling against the wall went to a hatch. "Two arrivals," he shouted. "One for the narcotics block. One for the muggers."

Another guard in the office unlocked the handcuffs and pushed Erim and Villi out into a dimly lit corridor which stretched far into the distance. They stood and rubbed the circulation back into their wrists, savouring their first unchained, unsupervised moments since arriving at the prison. A kind of freedom.

Whistling cheerfully, a young boy appeared out of the gloomy depths of the corridor. "Sheytan Villi," the boy grinned, "you weren't out long enough to piss yourself." "Shut yer mouth kid," Villi snarled. "Show my mate to the muggers' block."

Erim followed the boy up the corridor until he stopped before an iron door. The guard who slouched outside unlocked the padlocks fastening the door and nodded Erim to enter.

As Erim stepped into the block, he recoiled instinctively from the sounds and smells.

It was a two-floored block. Erim learnt immediately that petty criminals and newcomers like him were generally confined to the bottom floor. An old man pressed a worn, dirty blanket into his hands and pushed him towards a large, crowded room. "You're in there," he wheezed. "Find somewhere to kip." The bustle and echoing shouts reminded Erim of a railway station waiting hall.

Erim's first night was spent under the stairs, squeezed into an airless corner beside a scrawny man whose face was covered with barely-healed scars. "I'm Hassan, the knife artist," he welcomed Erim. "If you think my face is bad, you should see what I did to the other guy."

Hassan took Erim upstairs to show him the only toilet. Erim glimpsed the interior of a dormitory with bunks and lockers. It seemed clean and quiet. "That's heaven," Hassan explained dourly. "You've really got be somebody or have a long sentence to live there. Either that or pay Abdullah Chitin five thousand lire." Hassan grinned and went on, "You're better off beside me. At least we're right where the food pots arrive."

By the morning of the third day, Erim was exhausted. Hassan and some of his friends had been gambling and kept him awake all night. He itched from insect bites. The prison swill was uneatable and he was hungry. He was in a foul mood as he joined the queue to use the toilet.

"After me, kid," snarled a prisoner pushing in front, just as Erim reached the toilet area. Erim couldn't control his anger. His punch owed more to pent-up frustration than technique. The queue-jumper, caught by surprise, sprawled back into the urinal.

The prisoner stood up, bleeding profusely from a split

lip and holding a strip of jagged, sharpened steel. Erim backed away, his face white. He barely dodged the first lunge. A circle of prisoners, shouting support and lusting for blood, formed around the two men.

Abdullah appeared suddenly. He delivered a lightning kick which sent the knife spinning and swung round to slap Erim's face. "I run this block. If you want to fight, first you ask me."

He gripped Erim's shoulder and dragged him the length of the dormitory to the most private corner of "heaven". "You'll bunk here," he ordered tersely. Dazed and trembling, Erim said, "I haven't got the money." Abdullah smiled, "For you, it's free. From now on, you're my man."

Erim spent the first few days in "heaven" sitting on his bunk, watching and listening. He was handed portions of the same expensive meals served to Abdullah's pampered and privileged gang. The food was bought outside the prison and delivered by guards. Nothing was said but Erim guessed that Abdullah's generosity had a price.

When Erim's father visited, he was distraught. The old man hammered on the thick pane of glass separating him from Erim in the visiting cubicle, "How could you do it to me? D'you think I spent all that money putting you through school to end up here?"

"I'm all right. I've got a friend here," Erim tried to calm him. "Abdullah Chitin."

"Abdullah Chitin!" Erim's father blanched, "he's evil, that one. I've read about him. He's no good."

Back in his block, Erim studied Abdullah in a new light. He knew that he was a killer judged too imbalanced to be legally responsible yet not insane enough to be committed permanently to an asylum. He saw that Abdullah's intense, morose manner was abnormal. His flawless looks and obsession about dress, cleanliness, health and fitness, made him like a magazine fashion model – too perfect to be true.

But Erim came to see another side of Abdullah. However contrived, Abdullah's sense of personal honour and fairness stood out like a gleaming jewel in the bleak prison. His integrity was everything to him.

The two men sat side by side watching television. Abdullah dubbed Erim "The Professor" and teased him for his education and middle-class background with an undercurrent of respect and envy.

The other men in Abdullah's clique were élite figures from Istanbul's underworld. At first, they resented Erim's class and naivety and took pleasure in shocking him with stories of robberies, violence and sexual exploits.

But Erim enjoyed their company. His previously-held prejudices, that criminals were all mindless and amoral, were dissolved. Their rich, evocative language and strong sense of honour appealed to him.

One night, Mili Dai, an ageing cigarette smuggler, called Erim to his bunk. "If you're going to be with us, you have to smoke."

Erim, like other Turks of his class, viewed cannabis as a pastime for criminals and ignorant peasants. A drug associated with prisons where it was cheap and plentiful, sold by guards to supplement inadequate wages. Erim had resisted scarred Hassan's persistent invitations to smoke but he couldn't refuse Mili Dai. The old smuggler was a father-figure in the block, the only member of Abdullah's gang with whom he felt totally comfortable.

Erim sat in the circle of men, taking his turn to puff on fat joints. A tape-player wailed music in the background. He relaxed. Now he belonged. Abdullah and his friends let their suspicions fade. Smoking became a nightly ritual.

Jeans and t-shirt, Erim's uniform of youth, were discarded. Instead, he borrowed smart suits from Abdullah. Swaggering down the corridors with his new friends, Erim felt proud and alive. When Abdullah called at other blocks to visit gangster friends, Erim slouched behind him, revelling in the role of bodyguard.

He picked up the gestures and expressions of the men. It was a new language that led to new relationships. He felt powerful and important sensing the fear of the other prisoners as he passed in the company of Abdullah.

Head Guard Salih and his assistant, Yilmaz, couldn't afford to refuse Abdullah's generous tips and were always anxious to do him favours in the hope of a reward. To his face they were polite, even subservient, but secretly they dreamed of cutting him down to size.

Abdullah sensed it, but being polite and friendly to the guards was essential to keep up his comfortable lifestyle behind bars. Money in prison was useless without guards willing to buy or deliver whatever was needed. The game of mutual deceit was a convenience.

Erim was a novice at prison intrigues but his friend-ship with Abdullah meant that he also was treated with deference by the guards.

Erim served three months and was released on the same day Abdullah was transferred to Bakirköy Mental Asylum. Abdullah was released two days later. His lawyers used the psychiatric report to cancel a two-year sentence for possession of a pistol.

Outside, Erim and Abdullah shared an apartment. The two men were often seen together on Istanbul's nightclub circuit. The rise of "The Professor" in the criminal fraternity was a hot item for the underworld newspaper columnists. Erim saved the newspaper cuttings and photographs in his wallet. He enjoyed the notoriety of being Abdullah's bodyguard, weapon-carrier and debt collector.

He was the risk-taker of the partnership, addicted to the excitement and danger, and was often remanded for short periods charged with assault or extortion. Then he was convicted for possessing a gun and given a one-year sentence.

A week before his release, Erim saw his name on the visiting list handed through the block door. He didn't recognize the tired-looking, bent figure resting his head on the thick sheet of glass in the visiting booth. When the man looked up, Erim saw it was his father.

His father's eyes were moist with tears. "Why didn't you call to see us? Your mother..." He was too choked with emotion to continue.

Erim held out his hand but met only the cold glass wall. "I was planning to. First I needed money to show you."

"Money! Why? We had enough to get you through college." The pained voice became touched with hope. "We could still do it."

Erim turned. A prisoner approached him, his hands hanging crossed in a gesture of supplication. "Professor... Can I ask a favour?"

Erim waved his hand at the prisoner to wait and swung back to see his father walking away. He stood watching, wanting to call out to him but scared to show any weakness before the prisoner.

On the day of Erim's release, Abdullah was waiting outside the prison in his new Mercedes. When Erim stepped through the gate, Abdullah opened the back door of the car and thrust a lighted joint in Erim's hands. "I promised you I'd be here."

Three months later, Erim was escorted by police

back to the prison, handcuffed to a shivering teenager. As usual Salih gushed feigned friendship. "Professor Effendi, you're looking well."

Salih added another sheet to Erim's bulky dossier and they drank tea. He interrupted the small talk to ask Erim, "Who's the kid you came with?"

Erim glanced at the nervous, ragged figure standing in a corner, watching them with wide eyes.

"Nobody." He snapped open his gold cigarette case. "Sling him in the cage for the night."

Nahim's revenge

I first met Nahim in Burhaniye, an old country jail originally built for the workers of a nearby brick factory. Forty or more men shared each dormitory, sleeping on platforms stacked to the ceiling. Usually we had a civilized, ashtray-wide gap between our mattresses but there were times of overcrowding when even that vanished.

Nahim and I were both long-termers and it made for an automatic bond between us. A week after we met I became his "food sharer" which formalized our friendship. It was a tough prison, run on traditional discipline. A mistake earned a black mark in the head guard's file, six marks meant a beating. Nahim had suffered only one beating but that had been enough. When any guard, soldier or prison official gave him an order, whatever his thoughts, he never argued.

Nahim's lined face and gnarled hands attested to years of toil. Beneath bushy brows, his eyes slanted mournfully. A moustache straggled over his lip, ineffectually concealing missing teeth. He was no older than forty, yet his muscular frame was already stumpy and bent like an old man's. Only his wiry, black hair suggested youth.

His story was tragic and familiar. Throughout a twenty-year stint as a Mercedes plumber in Stuttgart,

Nahim had channelled every spare mark from his wages to his wife back in Turkey. She had invested the money, buying a little villa together with a small plot of land. Adjoining the property was a farm owned by a family which included two lawyers and a court clerk. Nahim was westernized enough to have overlooked a single springtime indiscretion, but his wife had become enmeshed in a full-blown affair. The day Nahim received his retirement watch, his wife moved in with the court clerk, taking every mark Nahim had saved.

"And it was all done legally. She sold the villa and pocketed the money," he fumed. "I paid the top lawyer in Izmir to discover that."

Together with a cousin, Nahim had called on the court clerk, carrying a shotgun to demand his money back. Believing promises given by the clerk, they had left empty-handed. Days later, a small amount of hashish was found in his car by police acting on information provided by Nahim's wife.

Hauled into court and ranged against the two lawyers and the clerk, Nahim was guilty from the start. His wife had also appeared to testify that Nahim had forced her into a life of addiction. Nahim and his cousin were sentenced to sixteen years each. According to their lawyer, they were lucky not to get life.

I met him as he was finishing his third year behind bars. His bitterness had tapered off into a whimsical, self-deprecating humour. When he talked, he had the intriguing habit of jumping from topic to topic along the slimmest and most tenuous links. It turned our conversations into bewildering dialogues of the deaf. There was only one constant theme, his pride at being a German-trained master plumber. As we sweated side by side in the brickyard, he whined, "What's a skilled man like me shovelling sand for?"

We swapped all our stories. Just as we were going to have to repeat ourselves, he was transferred to Izmir high-security prison. When I joined him three months later, Nahim was foreman of the prison plumbers.

He was a useful friend, always good for gossip and providing scrap metal for grinding into knives. Nahim called often at the foreigners' block on some pretext or other; it gave him the opportunity to show off his primitive grasp of German in front of his boss and the escorting guard. He had *ja*, *nein*, *Dummkopf* and *Schwein* off pat, and *Scheisse* he pronounced with full phlegm-spewing Teutonic vigour. As his ex-food sharer, my cell's plumbing was always in need of attention. "I'm a modern plumber," he complained, bashing the toilet drain periodically to pretend he was working. "I shouldn't even have to touch such primitive lead pipes."

Ali Ustah, Nahim's boss, was a retirement-focused civilian plumber, stuck in a suit and ordered to supervise someone vastly more skilled and knowledgeable than himself. Always diffident and respectful both to Nahim and to me, he relegated himself to tea- fetcher whilst we talked. The reversal in roles was so absolute, I wasn't at all surprised to hear of Nahim's promotion to Ali Ustah's job.

A few weeks after his upgrading, Nahim came to brag gleefully, "They've ordered me to re-design the prison's water supply and drainage system."

"I thought you were a modern plumber," I joked, "too good for this prison?"

His bushy eyebrows slanted indignantly, "That old Dummkopf Ali Ustah left it in a shambles. Somebody has to fix it."

He extracted a sheet of paper from his wallet with great care and passed it to me. "This is my master plan," he said, with evident pride. "This" was a greasy, crumpled exercise-book page, covered with spaghetti-like lines.

Throughout the summer Nahim was busy burrowing everywhere. Twice he appeared with his gang of musclebound cons to dig trenches across our courtyard. Compared to other blocks, we got off lightly.

But despite all his efforts and intensive digging, the plumbing didn't improve. On the contrary. The water supply during Ali Ustah's reign might have been erratic, but under Nahim it broke down once a week. It was a long, hot summer, so Nahim became a less-than-popular figure. Another year passed with little progress. To get by, we had to hoard stacks of plastic jerry-cans full of water.

Prison being prison, Nahim and his gang of slow-witted trench-diggers were the targets for the cruellest forms of humour. It was water off a duck's back. If anything, Nahim enjoyed the jibes. He had the enchanting ability to disarm the aggressive undertones with long-winded lectures on the drought problems of the Aegean region, concluding in oriental fashion, "I only direct water: Allah creates it."

Quite suddenly, Nahim acquired a new sense of confidence. There were small incidents that seemed out of character. A soldier, assigned the duty of supervising Nahim, criticized him for spending more time drinking tea than working. Nahim launched into such voluble histrionics, the head guard had to be called to pacify him. The escort backed down. "They have to side with me," Nahim boasted. "Guards and soldiers are like fish in the sea. A good plumber is as rare as gold."

He didn't abuse his position. It was more a question of knowing his worth and deciding to resist the nonsense of authority with its Mickey Mouse regulations. But still his changed attitude puzzled me – it was as if he had something up his sleeve.

Just after New Year's Day, he was locked up in the punishment cell. I never discovered why but I presume it was because of extreme insubordination. After two weeks lying on a dirt floor, cohabiting with rats and cockroaches, he was shifted to the remand block inhabited by the dregs of the prison. Quite a few guards and trustees taunted and jeered as Nahim staggered up the corridor, bowed under the weight of his mattress. I was probably the only prisoner to sympathize and I bribed a soldier to smuggle him a pile of German porno magazines.

A week later, when he stopped in the corridor to hand back the magazines, we were able to talk through the slit in the door. He stretched the process out to two minutes with some skilful theatrics. "A stupid Turk has stuffed paper down a drain," he moaned. "Now a man of my advanced skills is being called to clear it!" His delaying tactics at the door angered the pugnacious young guard who escorted him. "Get a move on," the guard shouted coarsely. "Talking is forbidden."

Nahim responded with an earthy quote from Nasretin Hoja: the Turkish equivalent of "You can take a horse to water, but you can't make him drink." When the guard prodded him to leave, Nahim growled, "You Turkish Scheisse Dummkopf Schwein." I laughed, with "good old Nahim – nothing has changed" affection.

Scarcely a week later, Head Guard Ismail summoned me to the administration block. As we walked briskly down the corridor, Ismail nervously pleaded, "There's no water in the Prosecutor's office. You're Nahim's friend. Tell him to stop messing around and fix it."

Nahim stood in one corner of the Prosecutor's office, arms crossed over his chest, stubborn, defiant. Facing him across the room stood the Prosecutor, hands thrust deep into his pockets, his normally bland features puckered with frustration and suppressed fury. Between them were the guards, standing awkwardly and strategically placed to prevent any physical clash between the protagonists.

"Talk with him," Ismail begged. "Not a single toilet works and an inspector from Ankara is due any day." Nahim turned to look at me. His eyes were slanted more mournfully than usual but they held a gleam of triumph and amusement. "They treat me like a dog – why should I work for them?" Nahim whined. "I'm locked up with psychos and perverts. Me. A master plumber. And I'm innocent!"

That was too much for the Prosecutor. His hand emerged from a pocket, transformed into a waving fist. "No one cares if you're innocent," he bellowed. "This is a prison and you're a prisoner. You'll do as I say, sleep where I say and behave as I say."

Ismail looked beseechingly at me but I could only shrug my helplessness. The Prosecutor and Nahim returned to their respective positions, glowering at each other. Fearful of becoming too embroiled in the argument, I slipped out of the office.

Nahim won. He achieved a transfer to the coveted trustees' block. It was a small building, separate from the main prison complex, where drivers and other privileged prisoners lived. This was not only a passport to go anywhere inside the prison, but also to take trips outside. Nahim also won the right to work, unsupervised, with labourers of his own choice.

With him free to roam as he pleased, our meetings became daily occurrences. He was an enjoyable partner for breakfast and afternoon tea. Plumbing breakdowns in our block became less frequent and repairs were swiftly carried out. For a couple of months we even had hot water for an hour a day.

One morning, our breakfast was interrupted three times by guards asking him to hurry. Finally Chief Clerk Hamsi appeared and wailed, "Nahim, you must come quickly. There's no water in the women's block and the Prosecutor is going wild."

Nahim glared at Hamsi, "Who does he think he is? I'm human. I've got a right to have breakfast."

As far as the Prosecutor was concerned, the final straw was probably an incident which marred the visit of the prison service's Director General. Director Gültekin was an austere, tall man, never known to smile. He peered out at the world through rimless bi-focals and was deaf to every complaint or petition. He was no friend of the foreign prisoners from the morning he caught them in bed during an inspection tour and spat, "Filthy, lazy heathens."

His annual visits always caused upheavals and friction as frantic guards bullied and harangued inmates into straightening the ragged humanized edges of prison lines. Washing hanging out to dry, pictures on walls, hair touching collars, a colourful bedspread – all had to go.

In the middle of the clean-up of the foreigners' block, Nahim appeared. His excuse was too flimsy. A leaking toilet wasn't an acute problem. It could have waited until after Gültekin's inspection tour.

Everything proceeded surprisingly painlessly. In one cell a curtain hanging, in another cell a three-day beard, but nothing serious enough to be written in the Director's feared black diary.

As a precaution, Ismail stood in front of the cell where Nahim was working on the leaking toilet. The inspecting officials were on the verge of passing when Nahim emerged, his overalls filthy, brandishing an excreta-smeared length of piping. The bodyguards jumped too late. Nahim inserted himself right in the path of the Director and thrust the pipe under his nose.

"Tell me, sir, what am I supposed to do with pipes like this?" he began. "Der Scheisse Schwein that built this prison must have been a lunatic."

Bi-focally magnified eyes narrowed. The delicate, haughty nose pinched in disgust. Seemingly oblivious to the storm he had unleashed, Nahim flicked the pipe and went on, "This isn't a pipe, das ist Scheisse."

The word "Scheisse" was accompanied by a fine spray of saliva that splattered into Gültekin's face. The venom with which Nahim cursed conveyed all the frustration and bitterness of his life.

For a moment, everyone froze. All eyes were fixed on the Director. His bottom lip quivered and the dreaded black diary began to rise in his hand. Suddenly, he turned on his heels and stormed out of the block. Our peals of laughter rang out after him right down the corridor.

Following Director Gültekin's departure, Nahim protested his ignorance and innocence. "What shameful behaviour? Me? Disrespectful! Never." He didn't convince anybody. We were fearful there would be repercussions.

A week later, I met Nahim in the corridor where he introduced me to an intelligent-looking, earnest young man. "This is Husni. He's the new prison engineer. I'm showing him how my water and drainage system works."

If the Prosecutor's plan was to extract Nahim's secrets before displacing and punishing him, it failed miserably. Nahim had built such a maze of pipes and drains beneath the prison that the young engineer left flabbergasted. Husni was followed by an entire team of engineers and architects who spent weeks striding around the buildings carrying stacks of blueprints under their arms. A few months later, their report confirmed rumours on the prison grapevine. Nahim's sewage, drainage and water supply system was both unworkable and unrepairable. A new system would cost millions.

In Turkey, the prisons receive the lowest of state budget priorities. Raising the money to replace Nahim's handiwork would take years. The fact must have been hard for the Prosecutor to swallow, but the Turks have an admirable sense of pragmatism. Nahim had proved his point. He was indispensible.

A year before his release, the Prosecutor arranged for Nahim to be given a full civilian wage and permission to take on his nephew as an apprentice. Nahim became very modest and helpful. He even acted in a friendly way towards his old adversary, the Prosecutor. Once I saw them laughing together like old buddies. Later, he explained, "We were remembering Director General Gültekin's visit."

On his release night, he visited the foreigners' block. I had several bottles of hooch for his farewell party. But two days after the booze-up, I was shocked to see him in the corridor wearing the same old smeared overalls. He grinned broadly. "No, I'm not a con any more. I've started my own plumbing business." Stretching his arms expansively, he said proudly, "This is my first big contract."

For more than a year, at least once a week he stopped off to see me, bringing small delicacies from the outside world. He told me about his divorce, his new car and, finally, about his new wife.

I went to visit him on my fifth day of freedom. The moment I stepped through the door of his office, he jumped up and hugged me. Grey-haired, tubby, wearing an elegant three-piece suit, he was the image of a successful business man.

He drove me off to his new house, introduced me to his pretty wife, who was half his age, and plied me with drink.

Taking me to a window, he pointed down the hill at a small, grubby building. "My ex-wife lives down there. She married the clerk, but now he's off working in the East." In a satisfied tone, he added, "She's all alone. I drive past her every day as she cycles to work."

Hassan's song

After ten years in prison, Hassan was a nobody – just a decrepit wretch, squatting in corners, staring aimlessly at blank concrete walls. Though Hassan was in his early forties, his hair was white, his mouth a toothless hole and his eyes had a frightened, hunted look.

It was visiting day. Dressed in baggy, threadbare uniforms, a line of prisoners waited anxiously in the newly-painted corridor. Soldiers watched them closely, ready to cancel the visit of any man caught talking or unsuitably dressed.

Ismail had been promoted to head guard but found it difficult accustoming himself to the position. He felt uncomfortable. Hassan's mother had asked why the long-promised amnesty wasn't given. He had no answer. Politicians gave promises and broke them without a thought to the suffering caused. It was left to men like Ismail to soften the blow.

Sprawled in an armchair by the gate was a young army officer. His fingers tapped idly on the grip of the pistol strapped to his belt.

The door of a visiting cubicle opened and out stepped Hassan. His face was white, his eyes glistened with tears. For a moment he paused and leant back against the wall; his head bent into his chest as he fought to regain composure. His mother had been more distraught than usual. Consoling her had been an emotional ordeal.

"What are you waiting for?" the army officer's voice snapped.

Jerked back into the prison reality, Hassan looked bewildered. Muttering incoherently, he set off down the echoing corridor.

The officer laughed, shouting after him, "That doesn't sound like one of your old songs, Hassan."

Hassan ignored the shout, walking without a backward glance. Feeling snubbed and belittled, the officer turned to the prisoners but instead of the expected sniggers, he saw a line of expressionless faces.

With a sniff of disgust he slouched deeper into the armchair. "At least that's one hard man we've silenced," he gloated to Ismail. His voice was intentionally loud so as to be overheard by the line of waiting prisoners.

Ismail's reply was so intense it was almost a whisper, "Yes. We've silenced him. May God forgive us."

The only sound was Hassan's footsteps retreating down the corridor. The prisoners watched the stooped figure shuffling away, holding *tesbi* beads by his side.

Once, Hassan had twirled those jet-black beads confidently, rotating them like a propeller to swathe a path through crowded prison corridors.

Then his thick coat had hung loosely over his shoulders, emphasising his bulky build. Black *shalvas*, with their spacious sack ready to catch the new-born Messiah, had covered his stumpy legs. His shaggy black moustache had accentuated the ferocity of his cruel, knife-scarred face.

He'd been a man's man. Both loved and shunned, admired and feared. When guards and prisoners had nodded respectfully to him, he had always replied with a gleaming, toothy smile.

The stories of his wild, violent youth lingered, passing

into the folklore of the prison. Facts were distorted and some more shameful episodes forgotten, but the nub was true.

Recounting stories about Hassan became an initiation rite administered to new inmates. He was so rough and raw, it was easy to let imagination ramble and transform him into a legend. To authenticate their wild tales, many claimed to be his closest friend.

But I really was there the night Hassan and a thousand prisoners rioted and flattened the massive iron door of the fascist block. It was the first time I ever saw gas canisters exploded by an electric current. I also saw the aftermath, the rubble, which was all that was left of the block wall.

It was after the fascists had killed "Whistling" Ibo, Hassan's friend. We had all liked Ibo, an old gangster with a tracheotomy hole in his throat, but without Hassan's leadership, none of us would have rioted.

He was like a lion. After the gas tubes exploded, he had charged alone through the clouds of dust into the fascist block. Alpaslan, the fascist block chief, pumped out bullets from his automatic yet, miraculously, none of them touched Hassan. There were broken bones and stab wounds, but nobody was fatally injured that night.

After that, Hassan became a high-risk prisoner, transferred every six months to a different jail. Like millions of Turks, I watched out for his name and photograph in the tabloids. The gossip column of *Günaydin* regularly reported his exploits from far-flung jails. His court appearances and jail transfers; the short-lived behind-bars marriage to a belly dancer. The night he hung a sadistic administration official from the top of the prison minaret by his heels and resisted capture for days, barricaded in his block.

My own stories about Hassan go back to the six

months I spent in his block, before his kamikaze attack on the fascists. They were of knife and fist fights, escape attempts and gambling coups. Only some bits were true but no one cared. I enjoyed telling them and newcomers enjoyed listening.

But no words could ever describe Hassan's music.

Istanbul Prison was run-down and neglected. Nothing could shut out the sordidness of our lives. Lice and cockroaches crawled, gagging smells rose from open sewers and hungry stomachs constantly grumbled.

But there came moments when the two hundred men, crammed into our block, were able to relax. Murderers, thieves, drug dealers and pimps, we would all lie back, close our eyes and let Hassan perform his magic.

Just the gentleness with which he fondled his *ude* and cradled the oval sound-box in his lap, softened the hard, muscular lines of his body. Then the first note would ring out, his stubby thumb drawing it from a taut steel string.

Hassan's songs reflected life with all its drama, romance and tragedy. He had the ability to give the themes a sense of urgency and credibility. His spontaneous compositions were in a language we all understood.

Hassan was not only a skilled musician. He had an astonishing intuitive feel for poetry, blending Koran passages with gutter obscenities. His biting wit mocked authority and regulations, ridiculed the court officials and prison administrators, and gave us strength to laugh at our desperate predicament. Prison themes crop up constantly in Turkish folk music but the authenticity of Hassan's songs gave them a special poignancy and impact.

His forte was classical love songs. He gave each one a depth and pathos that caused many a hardened, embittered man to retire under his blanket and weep. Late at night, when we lay searching for sleep, he touched our souls with those songs.

It was the apparant contradiction, that such a violent man could be so sensitive and gifted, which was the core of his attraction.

Anything was an excuse for a party. A birthday, a death sentence or an acquittal, it was all the same to Hassan. I remember the night he broke off in the middle of a bawdy, lively number. He maintained the beat with finger clicks, stamps and cries. Rising to his feet with outstretched arms, his muscles quivered to the rhythm. Then he began a Black Sea dance. Features puckered with concentration, strutting like a peacock, he moved with a delicacy belying the heaviness of his body. He swirled faster and faster until unanimously we roared, "*Haydi Hassan*."

His entourage of similarly dressed, appropriately named "mad bloods" dwindled, one by one. Accompanying Hassan was a dangerous practice which sorely tested the loyalty and devotion of his friends.

He was constantly in trouble yet, despite the beatings and health-shattering spells in the black, damp punishment cells, Hassan remained obtuse, pig-headed and charismatic.

Old cons showed me photographs of him taken when he was a teenager. Even then, his black eyes blazed dangerously into the camera. Over the years, although his temples greyed and the furrows across his forehead etched deeper, those eyes never lost their authoritative menace.

Hassan's popularity amongst the prisoners was natural and inevitable but the guards also felt an almost paternal fondness for him.

Turkey is a country where prison guards are disliked

and regarded as a necessary evil rather than as servants of society. Hassan's blatant criminality gave their work meaning and appeased their consciences. However corrupt society was, no one could deny that a man like Hassan had to be locked up. Like it or not, someone had to do the job.

The guards used him as a safety valve. When the tension in the prison rose, it was invariably Hassan who detonated the pent-up emotion. A fight, a riot, something would happen to arouse the men and provide a point of contact for the guards to sit down and talk with the prisoners. Afterwards, the jail would calm down and Hassan would be the scapegoat who cooled off in the punishment block.

The underlying truth was that they sincerely liked him as a man. He was a character, the joker in the pack. However many times he was slung in the punishment cell or subjected to *falaka*, being beaten on the soles of the feet, he always laughed it off and stoically accepted that the guards were just doing their job. In return, the guards made a point of softening the punishments, providing extra blankets on cold nights and ensuring the *falaka* strokes fell lightly.

The guards also admired his music and perversely enjoyed being the butt of his anarchistic, jailhouse compositions. At night, they often came to our block to listen to Hassan's songs of defiance.

As more and more political militants entered the prison, the guards drew closer to the familiar ordinary inmates. They empathized with Hassan's open disdain for politics. In a simplistic manner, Hassan was a patriot, dismayed by the political violence that gripped Turkey. His songs sneered at revolutionaries and nationalists alike. He sang that they were rich kids, too soft, too smart and too protected to understand real life.

The Marxists were mainly college students and had only imprisonment in common with the criminal inmates. With little success, they tried to influence and organize the regular prisoners.

After the riot against the fascists, many communist militants began to talk of Hassan as a proletarian hero. I once heard a militant prisoner sing a rather dreary revolutionary song he'd composed about him.

When Hassan returned to Istanbul Prison for a stop-over between Ankara and Edirne Prisons, the Marxists' lawyers raised his case. Normally, he would have spent only a day in the jail before travelling on. By appealing against Hassan's extra punishment, the lawyers succeeded in postponing his transfer. That same night, the Marxists staged a demonstration. They barricaded the main door until the prosecutor released Hassan from the transients' pen and installed him in a Marxist block.

Hassan was naturally flattered by the adulation of so many highly-educated young men. Despite his dislike of the political militants, he saw the advantages of having them as friends. They had money for extra food. More importantly, they had lawyers to delay transfers, protect him from *falaka* and the punishment block.

Hassan's dossier grew steadily thicker with entries noting his relationship with the militants. Ismail later told me he had warned him but Hassan took no notice. Thought for the future was meaningless, he saw only the present – to be endured and survived.

September 1980. The coup d'état. Hassan was thirty-eight. He had completed a fifth of his twenty-five-year sentence for murder. The soldiers took him with the first batch of men sent as punishment to Izmir Prison.

The army controlled all the jails and knew only the

information in their dossiers. From the moment Hassan arrived in Izmir, he was a marked man.

The Marxist militants had connections with important academics and journalists. They had lawyers working outside using every trick in the book to protect them. Hassan had only Ismail.

Ismail's career as a guard had begun in Istanbul. He told me he had known Hassan since childhood, having grown up in the same slum district. Ismail had transferred to Izmir Prison to get away from the turmoil of Istanbul but nostalgically clung to memories of night duties spent listening to Hassan's music. Like many of the prisoners, he had kept track of Hassan's escapades through the newspapers.

There was nothing Ismail could do to prevent that first beating. It was part of the routine induction process for high-risk prisoners. The soldiers were working-class teenagers. With their minimal education, they were in awe of the student militants and instinctively shied away from treating them too harshly. But Hassan was different. His speech and manner instantly identified him as one of their own kind. To their simple minds, he was a traitor who, by joining the militants, had betrayed his peers. They spared him no mercy.

The arches of Hassan's feet were broken during the *falaka* session. He was denied medical attention for three weeks and was left with a permanent limp.

Ismail went out of his way to be of help. He was able to assign Hassan to a block far away from the militants, into the care of a kindly rich smuggler. The smuggler paid for Hassan's mother to travel from Istanbul and live in a room close to the prison so she could visit regularly. He gave Hassan clothes and a beautiful new *ude*.

But it was no use. The punishment cell had not only broken Hassan's bones, it had crushed his spirit. The *ude* hung unused beside his bunk. He was never to play it again.

For a year the soldiers harassed and persecuted him. Newly-appointed officers read his dossier and called him out, "Come on, Hassan. Show us how tough you are."

Submissive and silent, Hassan stood, waiting to be dismissed. The officer sneered and turned to Ismail, "Look at him. He's half dead."

Ismail sighed. "Perhaps, but once his songs helped men live."

The secret policeman

I still feel embarrassed remembering our first meeting. He was crouching beside a pot of vegetable stew, ladling precisely equal portions into metal plates. It was a job that had been one of my clinic chores, so I asked Mehdi, "He's the cleaner?"

Mehdi clucked, "No. He's Jaffa. A cop. He guards this place." His tone was scornful, "A secret policeman."

I laughed. It was absurd. Secret policemen were supposed to be anonymous. What was one doing crouching in a cell of a prison isolation block, dishing out food for inmates.

And Jaffa looked up at me with such a wounded expression in his dark eyes, that he made me feel ashamed. I stifled my laughter and, smiling, nodded a greeting. The policeman frowned and turned back to his task.

Istanbul Prison's isolation block was set up for Mehdi and Hussein, two members of the Popular Front for the Liberation of Palestine (PFLP). In 1977, the two men had attacked Israeli passengers in Istanbul airport's transit lounge. The final toll was six dead and twenty-four injured. One small girl was paralysed from grenade wounds.

Less than two years later, West German terrorists hijacked a jumbo-jet and bargained with the lives of the passengers for the freedom of men and women, including Mehdi and Hussein, jailed in a number of countries.

For a week, during the negotiations between the terrorists and authorities, the Palestinians were sealed in a small cell in the clinic. As the cleaner of the clinic, it was my job to shop for them and bring their food. Although it was forbidden, I also brought them news of the hijacking.

Then German commandos stormed the plane and rescued the passengers. The Palestinians were transferred from the clinic to a block which contained ten single cells leading off a narrow corridor. Extra iron sheeting and layers of concrete were used to turn the isolation block into a prison within the prison.

The Palestinians wanted to use their time behind bars to learn English and they asked the administration whether Mike from Arkansas, Beet from Switzerland and I could share their quarters. The administration reluctantly agreed.

The two Palestinians were exceptional men with strong, youthful faces. Superbly fit and always immaculately clean, they were misfits in the prison. Only tangled, curly hair and shaggy beards spoiled their clean-cut image. But there was another side to them that I sensed from the moment we first met – a streak of instability. Istanbul prison at the beginning of 1979 was chaotic and dangerous, yet I still hesitated before accepting Mehdi's invitation to move to the isolation block.

I had a single cell, as much food as I wanted and no dawn head-counts. After three years of living in the normal jail, it felt like heaven. There were only we five prisoners and Jaffa in the block, so at night, when the juveniles in the wing opposite slept, there were periods of utter silence.

Jaffa's job was to maintain a twenty-four hour, seven day a week, watch over the Palestinians. Unarmed, as a precaution, locked up with two combat-trained guerrillas, his position was precarious. Thin and under-nourished, he looked like a teenage basketball player, all limbs and no flesh.

He moved in with the Palestinians only two days before me. Poor Jaffa. As the most junior intelligence officer attached to the prison, he was given no choice. His first actions were to fix a sturdy padlock to the cell nearest the main door which he elected to occupy, and to line the bars with sheets of newspapers.

He was like a frightened mouse. At any loud noise or shout, he popped his narrow head out through the food hatch in his cell door and peered nervously up the corridor. Late at night or early in the morning, he would open the door as silently as possible. First, he'd take an apprehensive peep. Then, if the coast was clear, he would creep out and scurry along to the cell used as a kitchen at the other end of the corridor. Our game was to catch him.

Lying in our beds, pretending to be asleep, the five of us waited to hear Jaffa pass. After he began to eat, we would go and stand in front of the kitchen door watching him as he crouched over, spooning food into his mouth. He would suddenly see us and almost choke with fright.

In the evenings, after he had served out the food, Jaffa tried to befriend us. No one gave him a chance. Standing around the kitchen, leaning against the wall to eat, when he tried to enter our conversation, I used to cut him dead, "You might live here but you're just a cop."

After he had returned to his cell, our sport was frightening him. First we would shout or drop a plate to attract his attention. Each time his head popped through the hatch of his cell door, Mehdi charged towards him, screaming wildly, and then laughed when Jaffa, reacting instinctively, jerked back into the cell.

Jaffa's sole interest that first week appeared to be food. Not only did he eat packed lunches delivered from outside the prison by guards, he also wolfed down large helpings of the prison stews.

All the prisoners eagerly awaited Sunday evenings when the kitchen manager emptied the shelves before restocking them with fresh supplies on Monday mornings. The tureens delivered to the blocks were full to overflowing with vegetables and sometimes even meat. On our first Sunday in the isolation block, over half the stew was left after we had taken our fill.

Jaffa had taken two helpings and was loading his plate with a third when Mike kicked the tureen under the table. "You don't need more. We're saving it for the kids."

Jaffa went to leave. Mike, the American, stood in his way. He was a small, hard man, embittered by six years in the prison. I took Mike by the arm. "Let him have it. The kids won't get it till it's cold and they'll only throw it out."

"Why ya sticking up for him?" He shook free angrily.

Hussein pushed the tureen out from under the table towards Jaffa. "Eat as much as you like." Mike frowned but kept silent. He was only a guest in the block. The Palestinians made the rules.

Later that night, Jaffa invited me to his cell for a glass of tea. I accepted, but as I sat on his bed talking, a degree of coolness remained. It wasn't so much the birth of a friendship as the beginning of a truce.

I discovered he was *lycée*-educated with a fair grasp of English and German. His Turkish chauvinism was predictable but irritating. Whenever I criticized Turkey, he buried its problems under tales of past glories.

But he made no attempt to disguise his disgust with squabbling politicians. The newspapers were full of their antics as they swapped governments every few months. He showed me a photo of the Interior Minister, scoffing, "I drew bodyguard duty on him once. I had to follow him when he went visiting his whore and gangster friends."

We had no real political discussions. The revolutionaries were then in virtual control of the prison and, to them, Mehdi and Hussein were Marxist heroes. We were living in their block so any openness would have been unwise.

Our evening tea-drinking sessions became routine. We traded insults based on our support for rival football teams and moaned about the cold. One night he talked nostalgically of his early career as a policeman in Ankara. Although his initial enthusiam at being recruited by MIT, the National Intelligence Organization, had ebbed, he was too honourable to complain. His job in the block was to spy as well as to guard. It was no secret but it would have been tactless to bring it up. Above all, he dreamed of his four-day leave. He kept a chart on the wall to tick off the hours until his first three-week stint in the isolation block ended.

Jaffa never really settled into the block but he gained enough assurance by the second week to spend the days lolling in the corridor, hugging the radiator and reading *Cumhuriyet*, a Turkish newpaper similar to *The Guardian*. We grew used to his company.

His role in the block turned into a Turkish joke. The main iron door leading out to the prison remained secure only when top officials were on the prowl. Once they were off the premises, all the doors were unlocked and the guards retired to the administration office. Their place was taken by political prisoners wearing red

113

armbands. Until the evening, when the guards returned and the doors were locked, Jaffa was the only civilian in the jail.

The politicals used the isolation block to hold revolution conferences. Every day, small groups of them arrived in their uniforms of jeans and anoraks. Jaffa kept up appearances, sitting stiffly by the door, eyeing them suspiciously as they trooped past him to reach Mehdi's cell.

Dressed in an incongruous dark suit and rowing club tie, Jaffa did his best to uphold the honour of the secret police. Mike, Beet and I took it upon ourselves to ensure that Jaffa never wandered close enough to eavesdrop on the discussions. He never abused the understanding. Come evening, it was back to the dinner, TV and tea routine to await the next day's performance.

Jaffa's first three-week duty-spell ended and for four days he was absent. After his return, there was trouble in the prison almost every day. The politicals preached revolution but it was the regular prisoners who caused most of the disturbances. They had nothing to lose and were too desperate to imagine a new social order. The old men sat glued to their bunks, waiting for freedom. The young "mad-bloods" roamed the jail dealing in cannabis, heroin and pills or gambling to make money. When boredom overtook them, they rioted.

The half-mile-long main corridor was scarred with sooty burn marks and graffiti. Every pane of glass in the windows and all the light bulbs had been smashed. Stripped even of paint, there was nothing left for the rioting prisoners to destroy.

A pill-numbed mob rioting is an ugly sight. They have no reason or fear and feel no pain. Often they came banging on the isolation block door, calling for the Palestinians. Jaffa, with our agreement, swung a thick iron bar down to lock the door from the inside. It always kept the rioters out, until the night a horde of them succeeded in levering the door open.

Jaffa stood in the open doorway beside Mehdi and Hussein. He was a hated representative of the secret police, a civilian spy in their midst with only the reputation of the Palestinians to protect him.

Calmly, Mehdi told them, "Why kill him? He wouldn't be missed. They'd just use his death as an excuse to slaughter us all."

The men gaped at him. One self-mutilated, drooling ghoul pinned Jaffa against the wall at knife point until Hussein gently prised him free. Jaffa, ashen, remained in the doorway, obeying his orders to stick close to the Palestinians. From within the block, Mike, Beet and I watched with fear, awed by his bravery. Mike whispered admiringly, "He's crazy but he's sure got balls."

There was a second riot, after which Jaffa vanished. None of us expected him to return. We were sure his superiors would realize the danger and futility of his job. But either they were blind or simply didn't care – after a week's absence he was back on guard duty again.

I was relieved to see him. The riots were frightening. Jaffa wasn't much protection but I felt safer knowing there was a secret policeman in the block.

The worst riot was the day the politicals' tunnel was discovered. The politicals, enraged that all their weeks of labour had been for nothing, began it early in the morning and continued right through the night. There was no moon, so when the electricity was cut the prison was in darkness. Shots echoed in waves round the courtyard as a cordon of soldiers outside the jail fired into the air to deter escape attempts.

In the middle of the night, Mehdi, Hussein and Beet disappeared into the main corridor. Mike and I convinced Jaffa not to accompany them and we sat around a solitary candle in Mehdi's cell. The entrance to the isolation block was wide open; all the block doors had been ripped from their hinges and hauled off to build barricades. Eerie lights played through the doorway as gangs of prisoners carrying flaming torches passed up and down the corridor. In absolute silence, we waited, fearful they would enter our block.

Finally it happened. A group of about ten prisoners swaggered in, hollering "Jaffa!" One voice clearly belonged to Adapazar Hassan. The obese psychopath roared, "Show yourself, Jaffa." In pill-slurred unison the men chanted, "Come and get it, Jaffa." We heard the sound of the padlock on Jaffa's cell snapping, then laughter as they ripped his bedding.

Mike snuffed out the candle and the three of us sat listening to the prisoners approach, searching each cell. Jaffa had to be hidden and the only possible place was beneath Mehdi's bed. Jaffa, the proud fool, at first refused to go and we had to push him out of sight.

Mike's action came as a surprise. Since the fight over Jaffa taking food, our friendship had cooled. The wiry, American smuggler ambled out into the corridor to talk with the cons. My first thought was that he was going to betray Jaffa.

"What do you want? This is the Palestinians' block," he demanded defiantly in crude Turkish.

Suppressing my fear, I stood beside him and added, "You're too late. Jaffa escaped this morning when the riot started."

The prisoners surrounded us, holding up burning bunk slats to light our faces and check our identity. One man peered into Mehdi's cell but saw nothing. Adapazar Hassan's scarred, bloated face was an evil, surreal mask floating in the blackness. "The tunnel. Jaffa busted the

116

tunnel." His numb lips stuttered the words mixed in a spray of spit.

They didn't stay long. The sound of an explosion drew them away. Mike and I exchanged victory grins while Jaffa crawled out from under the bed and carefully smoothed out his creased suit.

The next morning soldiers stormed the prison, using rubber bullets and tear-gas, and took back control from the prisoners. Once again, Jaffa was relieved of his duties but this time he didn't return. There was no need. The Palestinians were moved to the foreigners' block and the isolation wing was turned into a lock-up for transvestite prostitutes.

A month later Mehdi and Hussein escaped.

My article, published in the London *Sunday Times* three years later, was quite mild and fair. A few months after it appeared, I was called to the mail room of Izmir Prison. We called it the "art-shop" because of the felt pens used to delete suspicious phrases and words in letters. We all knew that the clerks there were really censors working for the secret police.

"Deny everything," Head Guard Jasim Baba grinned as he pushed me through the art-shop door.

Behind a table piled high with letters sat a man in thick-lensed glasses. Standing to one side of him was Jaffa. He had grown a moustache and his frame had thickened, but I recognized him instantly.

I took my cue from his expressionless face and ignored him. The studious-looking clerk/secret police-man launched into a predictable lecture, laced with threats. I apologized, explaining that because publication had taken so long, the facts had become outdated and I was now very comfortable in Izmir Prison. The censor mellowed and decided not to prosecute, despite my refusal to reveal how the article had left the prison.

In return I promised to write no more for the *Sunday Times*. Jaffa showed me to the door and, when the other policeman's back was turned, squeezed my arm and grinned broadly.

A week later I was taken back to the art-shop and found Jaffa sitting alone behind the desk. Jasim Baba stayed with me in the office so we had no chance to speak openly. In a bored, laconic tone, he read out a list of prison matters which I was forbidden to mention in letters. I hardly listened, it was so good to see him. He was confident and at ease, such a different Jaffa from my memories of the Palestinian isolation block.

"As you know, I speak and read fluent English. Because of you, a clerk has been disciplined. Now I'm in charge. If any of your letters mentions anything on this list, all your postal privileges will be cancelled," he ended, sternly. Only an amused glint in his eyes betrayed his real feelings.

I was on the verge of leaving. Jasim Baba was already waiting out in the corridor when Jaffa called me back and whispered, "Don't tell anybody who I am. I'm only a mail clerk."

I resisted the impulse to laugh and smiled my assurance that his secret would be well protected.

Jaffa's own loose tongue made the promise unnecessary. He confided his "secret" to virtually everybody and it became part of the fabric of jailhouse humour. We rated many cons as indiscreet as Jaffa, the un-secret policeman.

I had a hunch he knew exactly what he was doing. Unlike his studious predecessor, he was often seen walking in the main corridor and knew prisoners in every block. Willing to do anyone a favour, to collect parcels or contact lawyers, he turned into one of the most popular officials in the prison.

Jaffa may have been more cunning than he seemed but his popularity depended on actively playing the honest and decent character he portrayed. Buttering up the block chiefs would have been enough to gather information yet Jaffa was also kind to everyone. Leaving the jail to fetch a football kicked over the wall by the kids or buying hearing-aid batteries for an old cleaner hardly fitted the image of a ruthless police spy.

My own embellished account of Jaffa's bravery in Istanbul Prison made the rounds. Enhanced each time it was repeated, it made him sound like a modern-day Horatio. By 1986, he had become a father-confessor; someone to ask for advice about personal problems. He was willing to listen to anybody. However well-liked, Jaffa remained a man of the other side. There was always a border between what could or couldn't be said to him. His law-abiding decency ruled out any meaningful friendship with prisoners yet his manner of keeping himself at a distance inspired respect and confidence.

When he called me to the art-shop early one morning, I thought it was to talk about some textbooks I had ordered for the school. Unlike the previous visit, we were alone and a glass of tea was waiting.

He was clearly embarrassed, and it took a full ten minutes of hedging and equivocation before he reached the point. "I'm only here because I know English and German. They needed someone to control the mail of you foreigners," he began. I smiled encouragement and, looking away from me, he went on, "I haven't bothered to check any of your mail for years. I'm supposed to do translations of every letter you write but it would take too long. They'd never get sent." With an engaging smile he added, "I thought it better to trust you." I nodded my gratitude and Jaffa went on, "So now my English is rusty and next week my boss is coming. He speaks

119

fluent English." Blushing, he came to the point, "To avoid misunderstandings, could you help me translate some of your mail?"

I tried to stay serious. My afternoon was spent translating a bundle of innocent letters. I even added a couple of seditious lines and underlined them with the black art-shop pen. Jaffa kept his job, which might explain why Izmir prison remained the least troubled high-security prison in Turkey.

When I was collecting discharge documents from the administration office on the day before my release, I saw Jaffa in the corridor. Jamshid Baba, a crippled Iranian, was speaking urgently to him. Jaffa grinned as he joined me, "I wish you'd take Jamshid with you. Now he's got me taking his wooden leg off to be glued."

The corridor was very crowded and the only chairs were being used by two kids barely out of their teens. I didn't need to say a word. All it took was a cold, old lag's stare and an authoritative flick of a thumb. The two young cons jumped up immediately and slid away, looking resentful and frightened. Jaffa gave me a sad, disappointed glance and, sitting on one of the chairs, sighed, "There was no need to do that. We could have stood."

Taking out some bank notes, I pressed them into Jaffa's hand, whispering, "Tonight I'm throwing a freedom party in the foreigners' block. Can you buy me a couple of bottles of vodka and smuggle them through?"

Silent, he looked at the money. Then, shaking his head, he handed the notes back. "No. You shouldn't ask me to do anything like that."

"Come on Jaffa. It's my last night," I protested.

He gripped my wrist and with a penetrating stare said:

"You forget. I'm a cop."

The psychologist

"You'll do what I say because I'm the head guard and you're a load of convicts. Give up the Iranian and get back inside. That's an order." Jasim Baba huffed, "After all, he did insult a prison officer."

Jasim Baba should have known better. The foreign prisoners were in no mood to heed reason or orders. They crowded the entrance of the block, preventing the door from being closed, and shouted back an international selection of insults. *"Malaka", "Khowell", "Pidé."*

"They're like crazed animals!" The new young guard retreated nervously behind Jasim as the foreigners unleashed a cacophony of bleats, barks, moos and squeaks.

Jasim tried again. "Give up the Iranian and return to your cells or you'll all lose parole."

An empty threat. Prisoners serving such long sentences had nothing to fear from the Parole Board.

"Forget it Jasim. The Iranian has apologized. What more do you want?" appealed Dr Zeki, co-chief of the foreigners' block, with a bedside inflection. "He hasn't done anything worth a spell in the dungeon."

White-haired Jasim shook his head disdainfully at the young guard. "I can't. He's already lodged an official complaint." With a laugh that revealed his loose dentures he turned to me. "You're English. Civilized. Khomeini's only a little Iranian. Why all the fuss?"

Khomeini was inches under five feet, toothless and bald. His hangdog expression was so miserable, we all felt obliged to protect him. None of us knew his real name. He and an Iraqi had arrived together after being caught with hundreds of false passports. "I think that week I was an American called Joe," the diminutive Iranian would start one of his rambling tales. "No, stupid. You were a Jordanian called Abdullah," his friend would interrupt. To avoid confusion, we dubbed them Khomeini and Saddam.

Saddam was a jovial giant. His idiotic smile, enormous pimply nose and bulging belly were custom-built for slapstick.

He and Khomeini were ideal partners. They mimed an assorted range of characters and swapped wisecracks with near-telepathic perfection. Even when playing chess, their comedy routine continued. Cheating and bluffing, giving fascist salutes, spouting nonsensical harangues, wailing fervent prayers for drugs and fresh young virgins, the two army deserters brilliantly spoofed the insanity of the Gulf War.

But soccer refereeing was their masterpiece. They rushed around fiendishly, disrupting more than controlling, and turned our afternoon matches into hilarious entertainment. Saddam was outrageous. A goal was certain. The whistle went. All the players stopped, bewildered. Saddam, red-faced and panic-stricken, pointed to his throat, opened his mouth as if to speak and blew the whistle hidden in his cheek. Infuriating!

Khomeini reduced spectators to painful hysterics with his pugnacious attempts at disciplining players almost twice his size. All very crude and obvious, but we loved it.

Because of a new guard's mistake, was Khomeini to be dragged off to a punishment cell? It was unthinkable!

Jasim Baba had no choice. "That's it. I've tried my best." Shaking his head disapprovingly, he plodded off to fetch the prosecutor.

District Prosecutor Shefki Bey arrived surprisingly quickly. The expression on his pleasant face barely altered at the sight of the foreigners jamming the block entrance. Short and stocky, always wearing a crumpled, stained suit and polka-dot tie, he was Turkey's top penal reformer. Familiar with most of Europe's prisons, he often appeared on TV to argue his humanitarian ideals. Although highly respected, his only full-time job was to administer an approved school. But for two months every summer, when Emin Bey went on holiday, Shefki Bey also took charge of Buca Prison.

The whole prison waited for those months. Under Shefki Bey the whole atmosphere changed. Little things, like the arrival of well-stocked fruit canteens and Shefki Bey's tours round the blocks to talk with inmates, made all the difference. In some ways he was almost subversive, encouraging disrespect for authority by calling Emin Bey a political appointee with no interest in prisoners.

But Shefki Bey was no soft touch. Although always fair, he was a stern believer in law and order. He listened patiently, first to the guard, then Zeki. All the foreigners hushed and strained forward in the doorway to catch his words. Gravely he said, "Let's hear what Khomeini has to say for himself."

Saddam and Khomeini squeezed through the foreigners but stopped short of the corridor. Saddam stationed his enormous bulk between Khomeini and

Shefki Bey. The small Iranian poked his head out from under Saddam's arm. "I was doing my job." He gestured with his bald head towards the young guard. "That idiot asks me every day where I'm going with the stale-bread bag. He knows I dump it in the pig-tip," Khomeini spluttered toothlessly. "Every bloody day! He's driving me barmy."

The foreigners giggled with delight but Shefki Bey was serious. "That's his job. What did you say to him?"

"I don't remember," Khomeini grinned. The young guard advanced. "Effendi, he told me he was off to feed the ducks."

"Quack, quack," roared the foreigners as Khomeini blushed at the Prosecutor from Saddam's armpit. "And the trousers?" Shefki Bey asked calmly.

Khomeini wriggled his hand out from the crush of bodies and wagged a finger at the Prosecutor. "I was in the right. That ox told me to take them off because they weren't uniform." With a smirk and a lisp, he added, "I thought he wanted to thee my legth."

The foreigners let off a barrage of wolf whistles and shouted, "Get 'em off." "That's not good enough," Shefki Bey smiled. "Khomeini will have to come with me."

I stood beside Zeki in the vanguard of our foreign contingent, wondering if the time had come to hand over Khomeini for punishment. Then I saw the young guard standing behind Shefki Bey looking prim and self-righteous. "At least ask Hussein," I asked Shefki Bey politely, playing for time. "He saw everything."

Hussein, a mild-mannered guard and a friend for many years, winked as he passed me. "I didn't hear the duck remark," he reported to Shefki, "But I know Khomeini's a hard-working, simple country-boy. He misunderstands orders."

We kept the argument going for over an hour. Zeki and I sidetracked with complaints about conditions until Shefki Bey became angry. "You're in charge of the non-Europeans." He ordered Zeki, "Give up the Iranian and get inside." Zeki waved vaguely at the foreigners to disperse. When that failed to have any effect, he shrugged, "I'm only a prisoner. There's nothing I can do."

Shefki Bey played his last card. "This has become a riot. A military law offence." He turned to Jasim Baba. "Tell the lieutenant to bring his soldiers." His eyes roamed over the faces of the foreigners and he threatened, "Give up the Iranian. It's your last chance."

Our defiance followed a common pattern of resistance. Spontaneous uprisings were used to remind the administration that it needed our compliance and co-operation for the prison to function smoothly. The threat of military intervention was usually enough to stop trouble going too far. It unmasked the authorities' show of courteous civility and we were able to surrender with our honour intact.

The final act that day should have been Khomeini's peaceful exit to spend two weeks in a clean, comfortable isolation cell. The young guard would have received a fatherly lecture from Jasim Baba on rule-bending and Shefki Bey could have retired to the office with his authority restored.

But something went wrong. We continued to jam the entrance of our block. Even when Adnan and his platoon of helmeted, truncheon-packing soldiers came stomping up the corridor, we made no move to retreat.

Any Turkish prisoners with our history of trouble-making would have been split up and exiled to distant, far-flung jails. But government orders demanded our location in a single block. As a result, more than a score of the foreigners shared a decade of companionship, united against the Turkish authorities. We also had politics on our side. The career of one prosecutor had been ruined by diplomatic protests following the beating of an Italian. Even Shefki Bey had to think carefully before sending the army against us. The lieutenant bellowed at the soldiers to line up and face the block door, truncheons at the ready. I stood firm only because there was no way to move back an inch. Hemmed in by Zeki, Saddam and two hefty Greeks, pressed from behind by fifty other foreigners, I was stuck – mute – while a torrent of blood-curdling threats and curses roared out from behind me.

A single hasty movement on either side would have initiated a battle. For several dream-like seconds the foreigners and soldiers kept apart. Looking into the face of one teenage soldier, just inches before me, the absurdity of the situation was inescapable. He was so young and nervous. Between snarls, I winked at him and grinned encouragement.

The tension was close to exploding when the Prosecutor held up his hands in a gesture of defeat. "All right. You can keep the Iranian," he shouted, "but don't think the matter is closed. You're worse than the politicals. I'm going to transfer you all to Manissa."

Shefki Bey left first, then Jasim Baba and the soldiers. Only Hussein remained. Laughing with relief, we scattered to our cells and Hussein slammed shut the iron block door. But even as we swapped congratulations and savoured our victory, we were beginning to have doubts.

Manissa was a mental hospital notorious for turning strong men into vegetables under a regime of beatings, isolation and force-fed sedatives.

The first rumours of a Psychological Observation Programme reached us three days later. Aydin, a Turkish friend, whispered the news through the inspection hatch in the door. But after a tense week with no sign of any retaliatory action, we relaxed and life returned to normal.

On a Sunday morning, two weeks after the trouble, the door opened to admit a young, neatly-dressed civilian.

"Who sent you? What do you want?" We gathered suspiciously around the visitor.

The young man smiled. "I'm Savaj," he replied, "the prison psychologist."

He certainly had a lot of nerve to withstand the brow-beating we gave him. His good-natured wide smile sparkled with a full set of perfect teeth. Shoulder-length black hair fell boyishly over intelligent, sensitive eyes. He seemed entirely at ease, sitting on a plastic stool, surrounded by fifty shaven-headed men who studied him coldly. His long legs curled effortlessly under the stool as he talked. Shifting pain-wracked rheumatic limbs, we listened.

He had a Bulgarian accent but was obviously well-educated. His speech was dotted with jailhouse slang in an effort to sound familiar and friendly. "No mate, I'm a refugee. A foreigner like you. Shefki Bey wouldn't even give me an office. No one's saying anybody here is crazy."

He was patronizing and condescending.

Zeki and Abdul Aziz, the two doctors amongst the foreigners, grilled him. "I know. The Turks are barely out of caves," Savaj answered smoothly. "They don't understand the first thing about psychiatry." He laughed, "They can hardly read. Yet now I've been asked to compile personality profiles on you all."

We sneered at his efforts to ingratiate himself with us by disowning the prison hierachy and his adopted country.

Savaj's first visit lasted all morning. Old lags drifted away. New men, bored and wanting to practise their Turkish, stayed and pumped Savaj dry. No one took him seriously.

The next morning he was back. I was exercising in the yard and saw him sitting on a bunk chatting to Josef and Bayram, two Sri Lankan newcomers serving short sentences for petty thieving.

Later, over tea, I talked with the lifers about Savaj. Seeing him again had been unsettling. The idea of being "psychologically observed" disturbed us. We decided to ignore him.

He came a third time. "He's dangerous," Zeki muttered darkly. "Somebody has got to stick close. What if a new man tells him about our knives?"

Albino and I exchanged grins. Zeki's fear, that our knives would be discovered, was something we often joked about. The knives, an old custom in Turkish jails, were more symbols of authority than weapons. Although the guards knew where the block chiefs hid them, they were never found during searches. But I was curious to find out more about Savaj and told Zeki, "OK. I'll go and see what he's doing."

Savaj was in a downstairs cell talking to two Sudanese seamen arrested for selling drugs. They spoke little Turkish but Savaj's questions were simple. Name, country of origin, religion, education, training and family background. He asked the questions casually, mixing them with friendly chat. The seamen appeared to enjoy the attention.

His disarming manner and apparently innocuous questions suggested Savaj was a professional. It was disquieting. "Who's he after? Is he working round to someone in particular?"

We kept a close watch as he interviewed the newcomers. One night, as we sat around speculating on Savaj's motives, Osama half-joked, "He's trying to work out who should go to Manissa. What else would you do with a personality profile?"

No one laughed. We sat eyeing each other – wondering, suspicious. The first hint of paranoia.

In one of our regular football matches I clashed with Taymur, an Egyptian lifer. Was it a deliberate foul or accidental? I kicked him in the groin, he butted me in the face. "You should be in Manissa," he cursed. I yelled back, "That's the last match I'm playing with a maniac like you."

I took a long time showering after the match. It was mid-day, mid-summer and I had the cold water hose to myself. Thinking came easily. "How had the years behind bars affected us? Were we still able to think? Had we lost our reason?"

Back in my cell, I picked up a paperback. Whenever my cell mates, Dr Aziz or Albino, came in I looked up warily. I couldn't follow the thread of the book yet couldn't put it down. Over the next few days, every time I left the cell to collect food, letters or go to the canteen, I felt nervous.

The whole block seemed to be on its guard. Friends parted and locked themselves into spells of private introspection. Two Greeks, who had been mates for eight years, argued over something trivial and stopped speaking to each other. By the end of Savaj's second week of interviews, our survival instincts, alert to the slightest threat, jabbed out indiscriminately.

During Savaj's third week, he reached the first lifer to be interviewed – Taymur. Habitually taciturn and morose, suddenly Taymur became sinister and menacing. I tried to avoid passing him in the corridor. Uneasy questions kept me awake at night. "Why is Taymur so withdrawn? Is his self-control going to snap? God knows what that would mean. Does he harbour a grudge for that football fight? And what about me? How healthy is my mind? What about my own violent fantasies?"

It was dawn and I was jogging round the courtyard, desperately sticking to my usual routine. Breathing balanced, hypnotic calm. Suddenly, Savaj stepped into my path. "Would you join me for tea?" he beamed brightly.

We sat on stools in a shaded corner of the courtyard and sipped tea while the block woke. I tried to concentrate. Savaj asked me the usual questions: name, country, occupation, interspersed with sympathy and flattery. "Yes, I know it's the wrong moment to talk, but..." "You're an important prisoner here, so...."

He scribbled his notes in a tattered exercise book. When he paused to fumble for a new pen, I took a mental breather.

Something curious happened. Perhaps jogging had upped my blood count. A whole range of observations coalesced into understanding. Since Savaj's arrival so much had gone wrong in the block. Even the courtyard looked more bleak than usual, strewn with cigarette butts and rubbish, unswept since my fight with Taymur. Saddam and Khomeini had stopped playing chess. I realized I couldn't even remember when I had last talked to them. Sayed Ali, the effervescent folk-singing Iranian who ran the tea service, scurried past, head down, with an unusually sombre expression. Islam, the Afghani washer-man who sniffed the clothes we wore as he touted for business, was nowhere to be seen. His washing bag hung from the window bars stuffed to the brim. And there was Aki. Up at dawn! The overweight Greek, normally a nightbird, squatted sorrowfully by the courtyard gate.

Savaj was telling me the story of his escape from Bulgaria. He was probably the only cheerful man left on the block. All my thoughts crystallized. "Why the act?" I interrupted. "You don't see us as people. To you we're just cons. You're out to split us up."

It was all nonsense. Savaj believed in his job. I started to take it all back but Savaj stopped me. "Forget it. Sometimes I wonder myself what I'm doing here."

News of my outburst spread. Many prisoners supported my stand. They stopped me to say, "You told that nut-doc good." The men Savaj had first interviewed were his most bitter critics. They were furious with themselves for confiding in him and for taking him at face value.

The next morning, when Savaj arrived to quiz Albino, my Anglo-Italian cell mate, he didn't try to befriend him. The session was formal. Question. Answer. There was no distracting side chatter.

That afternoon we played soccer again. Saddam and Khomeini were funnier than ever. Spectators and participants roared at their stale whistle-in-the-throat sketch. No one gave a damn about the score. We filled the game with melodramatic tantrums, fouls and artistic goals.

Savaj's interview with Claudio took place the following day in front of a score of foreigners sunbathing on blankets. "I'm an anarchist Catholic," the streetwise Italian answered with a deadpan expression. "I was in Bulgaria once and both times there were sand storms." His rap had us in stitches. He went on and on. Savaj also laughed but took no notes.

After that performance, Savaj missed several days.

131

When he appeared again, he was in and out so quickly that we were hardly aware of him. There were a few more perfunctory visits, then he spent most of his time in the political blocks.

We were back to normal. Old friends were eating together again. Islam was sniffing armpits. Sayed Ali gave out tea and folk songs. Aki snored away the days. Hussein guarded the door and neither questioned Khomeini when he carried out the stale-bread sack nor asked why he was not in uniform.

Then Munir, the Pakistani lifer, tried to kill himself. It was the day Shefki Bey was due to hand back control of the prison to Emin Bey, almost two months after the mini-riot. The two prosecutors arrived at our block looking grim, Emin Bey tanned and fit, Shefki in his usual crumpled suit. "Show me the Asian's cell," Emin Bey ordered Zeki brusquely.

They waited outside the cell while Ismail and Jasim Baba, tried to persuade Munir to surrender his knife. We watched in silence. We could see Munir pressed against the wall, blood streaming from his slashed wrists. Ismail stepped forward. Munir stabbed himself in the throat. "Get out." His scream was deranged. "I'll kill myself."

Ismail stopped at the door and turned to Emin Bey, "What'll I do?"

Emin Bey hardly paused, "Get the knife. I'll send him to Manissa. He can't stay here."

"Give me a moment alone with him," Shefki Bey intervened. "I know quite a bit about him from Savaj's profile."

Emin Bey marched off with a sour, disgusted expression. The guards followed. We drifted away and Shefki stood alone in the entrance to Munir's cell.

An hour later I was walking in the courtyard when I saw Shefki and Munir come out. Strips of bloodstained sheet were tied around Munir's wrists and neck. Munir was talking passionately as they walked up and down the courtyard and I heard Shefki answer:

"But Munir, haven't you got a sister in Toronto? Why don't you ask her? For such an important appeal, I'm sure she'd send you the money for a lawyer."

The prosecutor

As Kemal Yildiz drives to work, all his thoughts are concentrated on a single inmate. Prosecutor Yildiz, "patron" of Bayrampasha, Turkey's largest jail, is an important, powerful man. He's tough and forceful with peasant-like features, wide shoulders and an immensely strong build.

Head Guard Salih Demir can guess Kemal's decision the moment he sees him stride into the punishment block. He's seen that determined expression before.

Not bothering with formalities, Kemal growls, "Open up. I'm going in."

Salih slams the key viciously into the lock but says nothing as Kemal enters the cell.

Kemal eyes the prone figure wrapped in a blanket, stretched out on the bare cement floor of the cell, feigning sleep.

Mentally he lists his doubts. Is it worth the risk? The guard might have died. Wouldn't it be wiser to send the kid to Sinop?

Sinop. The name terrifies. The looming castle, dating back to the Middle Ages, is the obvious solution. That's where all prisoners who attack guards should go.

The picture of Idris as a cheerful, cheeky twelve-year-old nags at Kemal's memory.

But Idris's stabbing of Nejmi was definitely a premeditated assault. If he isn't sent to Sinop, the guards will be right to complain. But what about Nejmi's bullying and provocation? Nejmi had a reputation for being too hard on the youngsters.

Kemal remembers his first meeting with Idris. He was the youngest member of a gang of street urchins, living rough on the proceeds of pickpocketing, one of the thousands of children who fled isolated Anatolian villages to seek their fortunes in Istanbul.

There were so many kids like Idris locked up in Istanbul Prison. Kemal often used to visit the juvenile wing to organize lessons. He liked their company and put a lot of effort into scouring the city for clothes and footwear, begging from the most unlikely sources.

He recalls with affection the time Idris tore up his clothes to make a ball and destroyed his new shoes playing wild, riotous games of soccer.

From pickpocketing the kid had progressed to burglary. During the intervening years, he had grown tall and muscular but his gutteral Kurdish accent and boyish features remained.

And then there was yesterday's stabbing. The first instance of violence. Kemal feels there is only one right decision. Indirectly, he is to blame for the stabbing. He should have taken more notice of Idris in the juvenile block. He should have spent more time with him. Now he has to heed his heart.

Kemal jabs his toe at the blanket. Idris looks up, his mouth curves into a sneering grin.

Kemal's spirits sink. Idris's face is swollen and bruised. His eyes are barely visible through puffed-up purple slits. His shorn scalp is criss-crossed with cuts and sticky with blood.

"Sorry. I can't stand." Idris's thin voice trembles.

"They were just playing with my face. Take a look at my feet."

Dramatically, Idris sweeps aside the blanket to reveal his *falaka*-scarred feet. The soles are black with blood and bruises.

Kemal turns away, his stomach churning. He gives Salih a scathing glare. "We had trouble getting him into the cell." Salih calmly returns Kemal's stare.

Idris barks a peal of barely recognizable laughter as Kemal looks into Salih's eyes.

With a weary shrug, Kemal swings round to face Idris. "Stand up. Don't bother whining to me about your feet."

Idris clutches at the bars of the cell and, wincing with pain, pulls himself upright. "So, it's your turn uncle. I thought you left the dirty business to the guards. Now you're going to put the boot in."

Idris makes the word "uncle" sound like a curse. Kemal speaks brusquely. "You were lucky. You missed his heart by a few centimetres. The hangman will have to wait."

"Not for long. I'll make a better job of it next time," Idris shouts defiantly.

Kemal ignores him. "The doctor's report and the guards' statement will show Nejmi's injury was caused by a splinter of glass. Don't think I'm doing you a favour, I'm just keeping a blot off my own record."

He stalks abruptly out of the cell. Idris screams after him, "You're a filthy liar. I stabbed him. I sliced him open. You bastards are all the same."

The sound is eerie and hysterical, the cry of a trapped, mortally-wounded animal.

Head Guard Salih stands by the entrance to the punishment wing, his face livid with anger. "It's not right. You're making a bad mistake. His age doesn't change anything. He knifed one of my men."

Kemal pauses by the iron door. He looks back down the corridor of the punishment wing, trying to think how to convince Salih.

It's pointless. Salih believes only in the old methods. Laws prohibiting violence against prisoners have no meaning. Even if he is able to persuade him, nothing would change. The prisons are too crowded and primitive to put humanitarian ideals into practice. Kemal faces the guard and speaks with a neutral tone.

"Shift him to the clinic late tonight. Do it after midnight so no one will see. Lock him in a cell at the back where no one goes." Kemal turns to leave but swings round to add an afterthought. "And Salih, nobody's to touch him again. If anything happens to him, I'll hold you responsible."

That night Kemal takes Idris's dossier home to study. He finds three rejections for a place in a modern borstal. Kemal falls asleep hating the anonymous Justice Ministry official who decided that Idris should serve his sentence in an adult prison.

Kemal arrives early the next day and sends a guard to fetch Haydar, the lifer in charge of the clinic.

Haydar is no ordinary prisoner. Gentle and refined, he was once a surgeon until, in a jealous rage, he murdered his adulterous wife. His friendship with Kemal stretches back a decade and has transcended a normal prisoner/administrator relationship.

Haydar listens to Kemal with an affectionate grin. "You're a soft-hearted fool, Kemal. I'll keep an eye on him, but it won't do any good. That kid is doomed."

Kemal doesn't see Idris again until he visits the clinic during his routine monthly inspection tour. Haydar accompanies him round the clinic, introducing him to the patients. Idris's injuries are completely healed and he sits glowering out at the world from an antiseptic-smelling cell. Kemal asks Haydar in a bored manner, "Who's this. Why is he locked up?"

Haydar shrugs. "I don't know. He's called Idris. He came here three weeks ago from the punishment block."

Idris flings himself at the bars, screaming, "You remember me. I'm the one who stabbed Nejmi."

Kemal gives him a scornful, puzzled look and moves to the the next cell. In a voice loud enough to be overheard, he orders Haydar, "Remind me to find out who he is."

Back in his office, Kemal summons Haydar and some of the other privileged prisoners who sleep in the clinic. "It's going fine. Don't allow anybody from the other wings to get near him. He'll have to stay locked up until every prisoner has forgotten about the stabbing."

Pacing up and down his office, Kemal continues talking, as if lecturing himself. "We need more time to convince him he's done nothing brave or manly."

The prisoners return to the clinic. They're the *effendis* of the jail, middle-aged, respected gangsters with a samurai-like code of honour. They take turns to sit talking through the bars with Idris. When Idris starts his boastful posturing, they cut the conversation short and drift away. Garrulous by nature, pining for company to alleviate the unremitting boredom of his bare cell, Idris is forced to stop talking about the stabbing. The old surgeon and the young burglar are worlds apart but Haydar goes out of his way to cultivate Idris's friendship. Each night they sit talking for hours, eating their meals together on either side of the barred cell door.

One evening, Haydar is sitting talking with Idris. The boy shakes the bars. "I've been here two months. I bet that bastard Kemal has forgotten about me. Sinop would be better than being cooped up here."

Haydar nods. "You could be right. The old geezer's got a mind like a sieve." Then he winks. "I've got an idea."

The surgeon walks away and returns with Yildrim, a stooped old safecracker. Haydar shows Yildrim the padlock on Idris's cell door. "I reckon he's right. Kemal has forgotten. D'ya think you could make a key? Just something to unlock it at nights but leaving it secure enough to pass Salih's morning inspection."

Yildrim crouches to study the lock. "Easy. I was snapping these before I crawled."

Each night, Idris is released from his cell by Yildrim. They sit together watching television. During the dull bits, Yildrim reads the newspaper aloud to the illiterate youth. Idris tidies the safecracker's cell as he listens.

Without being asked, Idris begins to help the cleaner who nursed his *falaka* wounds. After two weeks, he has a routine of odd jobs around the clinic.

Another month passes. Kemal stops in front of Idris's cell during an inspection tour. "Who's he?" Haydar is ready. "Idris. He's been here a long time."

Kemal moves to leave and Haydar continues. "He seems like a good kid. Why not let him loose?"

The Prosecutor stares into Idris's eyes. The boy's defiant glower falters and he looks down at the floor. Kemal sounds reluctant. "I've forgotten why he's locked up. All right. We'll try it out for a few days."

Head Guard Salih mutters as he unlocks the cell and flashes a threatening look at Idris before leaving. Idris emerges from the cell grinning and playfully punches Haydar. The old surgeon ruffles the boy's hair affectionately.

Five months after the stabbing, Haydar sits drinking tea in Kemal's office. "You're too cunning for your own good. I think you've done it. The kid's going to be fine."

Kemal shakes his head sadly. "Don't fool yourself.

He's doing all right in your civilized oasis but the real test is the blocks. Still, it has to happen one day."

A week later, Idris is transferred to a wing reserved for kitchen staff, separate from the main prison complex. Sayed, the guard responsible for the kitchens, is an independent, humane man. He runs the kitchens as if they are his personal domain, open to criticism and suggestion but tolerating no direct interference. Under his benevolent rule, there's an easy-going family atmosphere. Instead of the traditional iron discipline and rigid regulations, Sayed gains the confidence and co-operation of his workers using reason and collective decision-making.

The workers are predominantly young Kurds with a similar background to Idris. He appears to settle in with no difficulty. Sayed keeps Kemal informed when he brings him the daily sample of prison food for inspection. Sayed talks confidently. "I don't understand why you're so worried. He's in with some kids who smoke dope but he's had no fights. I was scared with all the knives around the kitchen but he's peaceful. A regular kid. No trouble at all."

Kemal spoons though the plate, hunting for stones and counting the number of beans. His voice is gruff. "I've been in this business too long. Even if I had it straight from Allah, I wouldn't trust the boy."

After Sayed leaves, Kemal sits back with a thin smile of satisfaction. Driving home that night, stuck in an Istanbul traffic jam, he bellows out a cry of triumph to the world: "I've done it."

Several weeks later, a boiler in the prison kitchen explodes. Sayed is severely scalded. The accident happens just when Kemal is about to fly to Ankara for an important meeting at the Justice Ministry. As Kemal hurriedly gathers the documents he needs for the meeting, Salih says, "I'm putting Turgut in charge of the kitchen. Just 'til Sayed gets better. He fancies himself as a cook."

Kemal looks up. He knows Turgut to be a hard man with a strong prejudice against Kurds. Certainly he is one of the guards who beat up Idris. The clock ticks loudly as he stares at the guard. Frowning, he moves to the door. "I suppose it'll be all right for a few days. Tell him to go easy on the kitchen boys."

A week passes. Kemal sits at his desk staring bleakly at the report. In retrospect, he sees his mistake. It was inevitable Turgut and Idris would clash. Hating himself, he screws up the report and hurls it towards the waste-paper basket. It's all too late. Turgut is in hospital with serious knife wounds, Idris in Sinop Prison awaiting a further sentence for attempted murder – a target for the vengeance of the most sadistic guards in Turkey.

A light tap sounds on the door and a young prisoner enters, holding a dossier. Kemal reads through the contents. Suddenly he slaps the dossier on the desk and rises to his feet.

Stepping through the punishment block door, Kemal senses Salih's accusing thoughts. First Nejmi, now Turgut. Kemal walks on until he hears someone sobbing and pauses outside a cell containing a blanket-wrapped figure. "Who's that?" he asks Salih curtly.

"A thief. Caught carrying a knife last night," is Salih's terse response.

The sobbing ceases and a bloated, bruised face peers out at Kemal with terrified eyes.

Kemal gives his order to Salih.

"Open up. I'm going in."

The priest and the preacher

At our first meeting, I thought John was a consul. In his late forties, he oozed worldly wisdom – the hallmark of British diplomats in the Third World.

He was a slim man wearing a Russian-style astrakhan hat and a knee-length fur-trimmed coat. In speech, complexion and build he was unmistakably English. "Actually, Welsh," he confided. A straw-coloured beard sprouting haphazardly and red cheeks gave him a cheering appearance.

It didn't occur to me that his companion, Anton, could be anything but a locally-hired bodyguard or chauffeur. His English was quite good but not nearly as fluent as his Turkish, Italian or Greek. He glinted gold from ringed fingers to amuleted throat and was clothed in a form-hugging Mediterranean-style suit.

My confusion lasted for two months until John visited the prison wearing a clerical collar and asked if we wanted an Easter service. He had never mentioned religion or given any clue that he was a priest. Learning that Anton was the real consul, caught me off balance.

Having suffered five years of consular sympathy without action, I mistrusted consuls. Although I was never openly rude to John, our relationship had been cool and distant. On the other hand, I had warmed to Anton.

After the Easter shock, I tried to switch my antago-
nism to Anton, who appeared not to notice. Together
with the other British prisoner, Albino, I met John
and Anton once a week in the room normally used by
lawyers. During one visit, I told John about the mix-up.
He grinned, "Don't be hard on Anton. He tries his best."

At Christmas, John and Anton did us proud. With
money sent by the ambassador and expatriates in Ankara, they bought us a magnificent parcel. Nescafé, mince,
chocolates, sauces, a dazzling array of goods. Albino and
I shared it out amongst the foreigners and for a week
we were satiated with tastes normally forbidden in the
prison. On New Year's Eve, tanked up with hooch, we
threw some rousing verses of "Rule Britannia" into our
international sing-song.

I began to look forward to the visits as an opportunity
to relax and to have conversations in English.

Though a loyal Anglican, John had a curious and
questing mind. We shared a mutual fascination for
the entire spectrum of comparative religions and
philosophies. This interest, coupled with our observations of the pervasive Islamic influence in Turkey, led to
many stimulating conversations.

When I asked John to help me smuggle my writings
out of the prison, he agreed very reluctantly. The first
attempt was far from easy. With a thick envelope hidden
down the front of my trousers, I walked awkwardly to
the administration office. The guards were quite sloppy
but the soldiers searched everything.

The visiting area was a small room with a desk and
half a dozen hard chairs. Every visit was overseen by
at least two soldiers and a guard. John and Anton were
made to sit on one side of the desk. Albino and I sat on
the other side, squeezed against the wall. As casually as
possible, I extracted the envelope from my trousers and

held it out of sight between my knees. John disgorged a mountain of papers from his briefcase and spread them out on the desk, as if searching for something. When the moment seemed right, I slid the envelope onto the desk top. Then John scooped all the papers together like a three-card trickster, and, together with my envelope, returned them to his briefcase.

We both became quite slick at making the transfer. John appeared to enjoy the danger. Even after one of my smuggled articles was published in the *Sunday Times* and the administration was investigating how it bypassed the censor, my letters still reached England.

It was months before John asked to read my work. Much later, he admitted to being another spare-time writer and brought some of his own poems with him. They were so sensitive and full of feeling, I felt privileged to read them. From that point on, we became close friends. Each week his visit began with the question, "What have you been writing?"

As time passed, John noticed the difficulties the guards and soldiers had coping with so many visiting consuls and priests. They were bewildered as to why Spaniards, Frenchmen and Italians, Greeks, Germans and Britons, all saw different clerics. During one chaotic Easter visit, with four priests simultaneously conducting services, Jasim Baba entered the room, scratched his head and asked me, "How many Jesus's were there?" The confusion was compounded by the inability of the guards to understand which prisoner belonged to which country.

Each week, John began to add new names to the list of British subjects to be called out for the visit. First it was Akis, the amiable overweight Greek, then a couple of Egyptians. Within six months, he had bestowed honorary British citizenship on half the block.

And it didn't stop there. Father Michaeli, the Catholic priest, and Franco, the Italian consul, joined the game. They timed their visits to coincide with those of John and Anton. Sometimes as many as fifteen foreigners, gabbling in five languages, plus consuls, priests and half a dozen guards and soldiers, were all crammed into that tiny room. The overcrowding and impromptu party atmosphere undermined all attempts to maintain jailhouse discipline.

However, John's master-stroke was the women.

After listening to our lonely, frustrated bleats he had an idea which must have taken considerable guile and organization to realize. First, a succession of prim NATO wives plucked from John's parish began to accompany him. Then he started to appear with young, often beautiful, travellers he'd met as they were passing through Izmir. The British consular visiting list turned into an endless source of jokes, full of sexual innuendo, for the prisoners. One morning, Jane from Bristol kissed Ali Baba's wrinkled cheek to say goodbye. The toothless old Egyptian immediately cupped his cheek, as if to preserve the sensation, and wailed, "Allah. My heart is broken." Even the guards contributed to the chorus of wolf-whistles and cheers as we carried Ali shoulder high back to the block.

John's voice held a note of hesitancy when he introduced Pat. She was clearly different from the other women. Unlike most first-time visitors, who nervously peered round at the bars, guards and soldiers, Pat was quite relaxed, sitting beside John. She was an attractive American with soft hazel eyes that would blaze accusingly when annoyed by our sexist humour. I tried to put her at ease asking, "He didn't pick you up on the street, did he?"

John interrupted, flustered. "No. It was nothing like

that." Pat grinned across the desk at me. "He's embarrassed. I told him two minutes ago I'm a 'born again'
Christian."

Her candour was refreshing. She sat opposite me, her
look direct and penetrating and in quick succession, told
me of her divorce, descent into alcoholism and, finally,
how she had been saved by rediscovering Jesus. "Don't
you sometimes wonder if being stuck here goes back to
your denial of Jesus?" she asked me seriously.

Her question infuriated me. I was on the verge of
condemning Christianity for every evil under the sun,
from heretic-burning to genocide. Then I caught John's
eye, pleading with me to be gentle. Fortunately, it was
the moment Jasim Baba shouted that the visit was over.
As she was leaving, Pat whispered urgently, "Think
about it and tell me your answer next week."

Pat's question disturbed me. It was the kind of
question that threw up different answers each time I
looked at it. A week later, at their next visit, I was still
searching for a reply. As usual, John asked, "What have
you been writing?"

"Nothing." I paused, then said, "I've been thinking
about that Jesus question."

John and Pat exchanged glances. With a hint of
sarcasm, John asked her, "Are you satisfied?"

Pat ignored him and leaned over the desk, smiling
at me warmly. "Don't worry. It'll pass," she said. "If you
ever manage to answer the question you'll be writing
better than ever."

During the following visits, Pat met the other foreigners. Zeki, the devout, bible-reading Muslim doctor,
became her favourite. I spent more time with John.

The visits were busy. Information gathered and
imparted. The shoe and shirt sizes of fifty imprisoned
kids listed, to ensure they wouldn't shiver through

winter. My first manuscript compiled. Documents to be copied. Bank receipts signed and dental debts paid. So much to communicate and so little time.

After one hectic exchange of messages, John and I looked across the room at Pat. She was simultaneously fending off Nico's amorous advances, answering the Sri Lankan's missing-cheque related questions and explaining a new batch of Bible tracts to Zeki.

"She appears to be settling in," I said cheerfully.

John nodded. "Yes, she achieves a lot." Seemingly to himself, he muttered dejectedly, "But she doesn't think the same of me."

I was worried. Studying him carefully, I realized he was looking haggard. Something had happened and it was linked with Pat. I tried everything from subtle questions to interrogation but John was too evasive and discreet to give me a single clue.

I puzzled over the mystery even after returning to the block and, drinking tea with Sayed Ali from Tabriz, tried to talk it through. Sayed only sneered, "What's it to you? We're serving life here. Even if the Ayatollahs are stabbing each other out there, it's not our problem."

It wasn't until late at night that I saw the flaw in Sayed's reasoning. That the argument between John and Pat stemmed from a clash of religious opinions, was incidental. I was worried about the physical health of my friend, not his spiritual beliefs.

I didn't have to wait long for more news. The thousand-odd westerners living in Izmir were a tiny, isolated community. Foreign prisoners were locked away but still received their fair share of expatriate gossip. The Greek consul was the first to report but his early story lacked the details of Father Michaeli's later version.

The plump Italian was incensed by Pat's behaviour.

148

Not only had she been arrested for preaching to the Turks, she had done it in John's church. Scandal had been narrowly averted by Anton, who had used connections to get the charges dropped. She had shamed the entire community and endangered sixty years of Christian/Muslim harmony. I found the idea of Pat being locked up in the women's block momentarily entertaining but, without a dramatic dénouement, the event was quickly forgotten.

Nothing really changed and the visits continued as normal. Pat's brief arrest was never talked about. There was plainly an undercurrent of ill-feeling between her and John but they remained civil and polite to each other. She found a job tutoring the children of the regional prosecutor and somehow he wangled her a pass to visit the foreigners virtually whenever she liked. Living just around the corner from the prison, she was always dropping in for a quick chat on her way to or from town.

Most of her business at the prison centred on helping prisoners from Egypt, Iran, Pakistan and India. They had no consulates or money, so her minute favours were intensely appreciated. A pack of flints for Khomeya the lighter repairer or a couple of bladders for Sardar the football-maker cost next to nothing, yet provided tobacco, tea and self-respect for a month. She gave more help to those who needed it than any other prison visitor.

I knew Pat had a private income but I was still surprised by her decision to settle in Izmir. When I asked her reasons, she answered simply, "I'm needed here." Unlike John and most of the other Westerners living in Turkey, she began to study Turkish.

Turkish is a simple language inasmuch as it has a phonetic alphabet and only three basic tenses. However, it's also a very strange language. English speakers have difficulty in forming the mouth shapes and mastering the inverted sentence structure. It took me a decade to attain fluency. Pat was speaking it well within three years. After one visit, Khomeya complained gruffly, "Today she asked me why I'm a Muslim. It's indecent. Her Turkish is too good."

During the spring of 1986, in the midst of a typically chaotic visit, she shouted across the room at me, "I'm going back to Kentucky for a few months. Think of anything you need and I'll call you out next week." Sure enough, early one morning a visiting slip was handed through the block door bearing my name only. Hurriedly, I dressed and was escorted to the visiting room. Apart from a yawning guard, there was only Pat.

She was looking very happy and healthy. Obviously excited, she couldn't wait to tell me her news. Waving a letter, she said breathlessly, "They've accepted. My church in Kentucky is going to fund a hostel for homeless women here." Her voice became subdued and full of awe, "I prayed for it and now it's going to happen."

We talked for fifteen minutes. At one point the conversation drifted to her relationship with John and I asked, "Why do you keep criticizing him?"

She was thoughtful for a moment and then said, "It's a matter of style. We're both Christians. John believes in the forces of history. He thinks that Christian action and example is enough. But I think that because Jesus gives me strength, I must teach everybody how they can lean on Him."

"Do you think John's wrong for not trying to convert Muslims?" I asked. Without waiting for an answer, I went on, "Can't people be good unless they're Christians?"

Her reply was an enigmatic smile. Then she rose to

go, "We'll talk about it later, when I get back from the States."

We never did have that talk. The nearest we got was when I was sitting with her and John in a restaurant after my release. I was still goggle-eyed with my three-day-old freedom. John was in sparkling form and, putting on a pompous headmaster-ish tone, asked, "And so, my son. After all our efforts, have you emerged a true and devout Christian?"

Pat and I looked at each other. Clearly we were both taken back to our conversation in the prison. Laughing, I answered, "No. It would feel wrong. I want to make it on my own."

This delighted John. Pat smiled but I knew she was disappointed. The next day, after a morning at the police station begging for an exit permit to return to London, I met up with her for a snack. Afterwards, we went shopping in a rundown district of Izmir for second-hand furniture for the women's hostel. She haggled expertly with the dealers and bought two antique wardrobes. After the delivery details had been arranged, we jumped on a bus to the hostel.

It was a large, dignified wooden building with elaborately-carved balconies. A dozen women were already there, cleaning and decorating the interior. They were joking together and singing Turkish folk songs. I was impressed. Pat had achieved something of value and importance.

An old woman put a wood chisel in my hand and I began to work, cleaning the carved relief pattern around a fireplace. I was physically exhausted from three days without sleep; my mind was racing. In the hotel, an *Observer* journalist waited and at the police station a prosecutor had just told me, "I'm sorry. You're only free on parole. You've got to stay in Turkey for another twelve years." I chiselled away at a hundred years of dirt to reveal the intricate design. It was soothing. One by one, Pat brought the women to where I was working and introduced me. They smiled and welcomed me to their home. As we all worked, light-hearted, friendly banter and singing filled the hostel with an atmosphere of joy and optimism. For the first time since my release, I was happy.

Pat took it for granted that I would eat dinner at the hostel and laid a place for me at the head of a large sturdy table. As I took my seat, a pretty young girl shouted towards the kitchen, "Bring him the pot. He needs feeding up." All the women laughed as they sat round the table and Pat joked, "What do you expect after twelve years of prison food?" Still bemused by the novelty of handling a knife and fork, I tucked in as soon as the food was brought, but Pat, standing behind my chair, put her hand firmly on my shoulder, "Wait a moment. We've got to give thanks." Then she began her prayer.

The women became serious. The speed with which the atmosphere changed was alarming. The women bowed their heads and, except for Pat's monotone prayer, there was total silence. Pat finished the prayer and the women began to eat, laughing and gossiping again. Pat looked round benignly. Her satisfied smile turned to a slight frown when an old woman cackled noisily. Something about the ambience suddenly struck me as oppressive and phoney.

Two days later, John invited me to dinner. Our simple meal consisted of boiled potatoes, boiled vegetables and boiled meat. There was nothing to remind me of the fatty jail food. Dinner was interrupted by a telephone call. John returned to the table, obviously irritated, but the only explanation he offered was the comment, "That woman thinks she's got a monopoly on God."

I was stuck in Izmir over the next weekend, waiting for my exit permit, so there was no excuse for avoiding John's morning service. I arrived early and sat at a nearby cafe on a hillside overlooking the church. It was an old building surrounded by a garden with palm trees, bushes and flowers. Stone for stone, it was a typical English village church. The sound of a bell ringing from the steeple revived memories which were familiar yet belonged to another, alien, identity.

The congregation began to arrive. They were mostly English and American NATO officers with their families. All of them neatly dressed, they walked upright and proud from shiny cars to the church. I felt inferior, unfit to join them and didn't approach the church until the service began. I dreaded the thought of entering.

For a moment, I hesitated before the open door. Then I turned away and sat on a bench in a shaded corner of the church garden. I was so distracted, it took some time to realize I wasn't alone. Two women, half concealed by bushes, were sitting close to me. One was young and pretty but her features had an expression of infinite sadness. The other woman was middle-aged, bent and worn out. Judging by their scarves and gaudy-coloured dresses over traditional *shalvas*, they were both villagers.

We eyed each other for some minutes before the older woman came over to me. "*Salaam alaykum*," she said, smiling. "*Alaykum salaam*," I replied automatically. Squatting on the ground in front of me, she began to talk. I learnt she was from a village near Edremit and the girl was her daughter. It was relaxing to slip back into Turkish. Thinking became simple and felt natural. She showed no surprise when I told her I was an Englishman just out of jail. Immediately she asked, "Then you know the priest here?" I nodded and she continued, "Does he speak Turkish?" "No," I answered, and added, "can I be of any help?"

The woman turned and said something to the girl who studied me with dark, serious eyes before whispering a reply. With a nod of agreement, the mother asked me, "If I tell you the problem, can you explain it to the priest in heathen language?" She looked at me in such a direct manner, I promised to talk to John.

With expansive gestures, using country expressions, the woman told me that her daughter's fiancé was working in Germany to earn the money to buy her from her family. A relative, also living in Germany, had written a letter home saying the fiancé was being unfaithful. Gripping my hand, her voice was hoarse. "A German priest has cast a spell to make him fall in love with a heathen." She showed me a sheet of paper covered with a childlike scrawl and described how she had taken the letter to the village *mukhtar*. He had advised that the only solution was to persuade another heathen priest to make a counter-spell. The girl stared at me hopefully as her mother asked, "Do you think the priest will ask much money?" I smiled and shook my head.

The service ended and the congregation began to leave. Each person stopped to exchange a few words with John on the porch before drifting away. Together with the Turkish mother and daughter, I hid behind the bushes until John was alone.

He listened carefully as I translated the girl's story. I beckoned her to approach. She froze for some seconds, gazing at John in his flowing robes, her mouth open. Then, she stepped warily, like a frightened fawn, towards him and stopped at the foot of the church steps. John reached out and rested his hand lightly on the girl's forehead. At first she looked so terrified, I was sure she would run off. Then her expression and posture relaxed and she fixed her gaze trustingly on John's face. Together with the girl's mother, I watched captivated by the scene which lasted no more than a minute. John smiled down at the girl to show he was finished. Her face lit up, her eyes widened. She radiated happiness. John stood beaming as the girl skipped away with her mother hobbling behind.

We said nothing walking round to the vestry. We were both feeling so pleased, we didn't want to spoil the mood. Only later did I ask, "You didn't really put a counter-spell on her fiancé?"

"No. I said a prayer for her happiness. What else could I do?" John's eyes twinkled. "You saw. It worked."